As Ryan turn_____ur himself another _____and snuck up behind _____ arms around his bare waist and _____ng her face against his muscular back. "You know, I've been waiting for this night for ages," she admitted dreamily. "Ever since the very first time I saw you last summer."

"Oh yeah?" he teased. "That's a surprise. You looked awfully busy with Ben Mercer to me."

Jessica stiffened involuntarily at the sound of Ben's name, then forced herself to relax again. "Ben was nothing to me—just someone to hang out with," she lied, hoping Ryan wouldn't catch on. "*You* were the guy I really wanted."

Ryan put down the whiskey bottle and loosened her arms just enough to turn around and face her. "I like a woman who knows what she wants," he said, flashing a slow, sexy grin. He put his hands on Jessica's shoulders and pulled her tightly against his chest. "I must have been blind to have chosen your sister over you."

Bantam Books in the Sweet Valley University series.
Ask your bookseller for the books you have missed.

And don't miss these Sweet Valley
University Thriller Editions:

Visit the Official Sweet Valley Web Site on the Internet at:

http://www.sweetvalley.com

SWEET VALLEY UNIVERSITY®

The Boys of Summer

Written by
Laurie John

Created by
FRANCINE PASCAL

BANTAM BOOKS
NEW YORK · TORONTO · LONDON · SYDNEY · AUCKLAND

RL 6, age 12 and up

THE BOYS OF SUMMER

A Bantam Book / September 1997

Sweet Valley High® and Sweet Valley University®
are registered trademarks of Francine Pascal.
Conceived by Francine Pascal.
Produced by Daniel Weiss Associates, Inc.
33 West 17th Street
New York, NY 10011.

ISBN: 0-553-57056-0

Published simultaneously in the United States and Canada

Bantam Books are published by Bantam Books, a division of Bantam
Doubleday Dell Publishing Group, Inc. Its trademark, consisting of the
words "Bantam Books" and the portrayal of a rooster, is Registered in
U.S. Patent and Trademark Office and in other countries. Marca
Registrada. Bantam Books, 1540 Broadway, New York, New York 10036.

PRINTED IN THE UNITED STATES OF AMERICA

OPM   0 9 8 7 6 5 4 3 2 1

To Marvin and Evelyn Farbman

Chapter One

I can only love him, Elizabeth Wakefield reminded herself, her blue-green eyes bloodshot and swollen from crying. *He's got to figure out his life on his own.*

Elizabeth knew she was right, but it was an amazingly small consolation. Only an hour before, she'd stumbled onto her traitorous identical twin, Jessica, locked in a passionate, steamy embrace with Elizabeth's ex-boyfriend Ryan Taylor; the sight was branded upon her mind somehow. She could still picture Jessica's toned arms wrapped around Ryan's bare back, his tan hands in her sister's blond hair. Just thinking about it made Elizabeth's stomach twist with nausea. She wished with all her heart that she hadn't gone to Ryan's room earlier that Wednesday evening.

"How could Jessica *do* this to me?" she wailed to her empty bedroom. The tears began again in

1

earnest as she threw herself facedown onto the already wet pillow at the head of her single bed. Unfortunately she already knew the answer to her question. The entire situation was her own dumb fault! How could she have been so stupid as to have told Jessica that she was through with Ryan for good—that she didn't care *whom* he dated?

On the other hand, how could Jessica have gone after Ryan so soon after he'd broken Elizabeth's heart? How could she have gone after him at all?

You should have known *she would,* Elizabeth thought masochistically, crying harder. Jessica had had the hots for Ryan from the very first day of the previous summer, when the twins had come to Sweet Valley Shore to try out for the lifeguard squad. It had always been a sore point with Jessica that Ryan had liked Elizabeth better than her; now that Jessica's last-summer's boyfriend, Ben Mercer, had dumped her for someone else, it made perfect sense that Jessica would make her move on Ryan.

In fact, a lot of things made perfect sense now. For instance, the reason that Ryan was acting so strange and distant lately, and the reason he'd given up his post as head lifeguard. He was drinking again—years of sobriety wasted in a single, stupid moment. Elizabeth had been so proud of his success in taking back control of his life, so hopeful for his future. But Ryan's Alcoholics

Anonymous sponsor, Patti Yager, had fallen off the wagon herself. Elizabeth should have known that Ryan wouldn't be too far behind.

"If only I hadn't missed his anniversary dinner!" She sniffled into the pillow, guilt crowding in to join all the other horrid emotions circling through her head. Ryan had invited her out to dinner with him to celebrate another year of sobriety, and Elizabeth had fully intended to make the evening perfect—a gift for him, a glamorous new hairdo for her, maybe a romantic walk in the moonlight after dinner. But Elizabeth had gotten horribly held up at the salon and then, when she was finally on her way to the restaurant to meet Ryan, her Jeep had broken down in the middle of nowhere. There had been no phone, no way to contact him, and she'd never made it to the restaurant at all. Ryan had been devastated. Elizabeth knew now that that was the night he'd started drinking again. She felt awful about it— untrustworthy, unreliable, and *so* irresponsible.

Being ignored and abandoned like that was the reason he fell off the wagon, Elizabeth told herself. *I totally let him down. And now everything's out of control.*

And the last thing this already volatile situation needed was Jessica Wakefield. Jessica was sure to be the spark to Ryan's gasoline. Jessica wouldn't try to stop Ryan's self-destructive behavior—knowing Jessica, she'd encourage it!

3

No, that's not fair, Elizabeth told herself, struggling to calm down. *You know that Jessica doesn't like drinking either. She's not going to hang around with Ryan once she finds out what she's dealing with.*

But how is she going to find out? a little voice in Elizabeth's head argued. You're *not going to tell her. You never even told anyone that Ryan was a recovering alcoholic—let alone that he's a raging drunk again.*

Once again the picture of Ryan kissing her sister forced itself on Elizabeth's unwilling memory. *Jessica will just have to figure it out by herself!* she thought angrily. *After the way she double-crossed me with Ryan, she doesn't deserve my help!*

Even as she thought it, though, Elizabeth knew that she was kidding herself. Of *course* she was going to have to tell her sister the truth about Ryan. It killed Elizabeth to think of breaking Ryan's trust by exposing his secret that way, but hadn't he forced her into it? She couldn't let Jessica get into a relationship so sure to end in misery without at least warning her.

Not only that, Elizabeth rationalized, *but if Jessica will do the right thing and bow out gracefully, maybe I can still help Ryan.*

Maybe I can keep him from destroying his life.

After all, she knew Ryan better than Jessica. Elizabeth had been more than a girlfriend to him. She was his *friend,* plain and simple. She understood the situation.

Oh, why don't you just admit it? Elizabeth asked herself bitterly, choking on her sobs. *You're still in love with him.*

"Yes," she whimpered. "Yes, it's true." And the thought of losing him to Jessica made her want to curl up and die.

Nina Harper fumbled with her key at the back door of the Victorian beach house, still in shock from what she'd just seen.

I thought this *guy would be different,* she reminded herself, almost dropping her key ring. *I thought that maybe*—maybe—*there was one member of the male species on the planet that wasn't a total loser. But no, I was wrong.*

She still couldn't believe *how* wrong.

Nina flipped on the kitchen light and trudged across the red-and-black checkerboard-style linoleum floor, heading for the staircase. The house was totally, eerily quiet.

Ben must be out with Priya, Nina thought as she passed his darkened first-floor room. *I hope Elizabeth's home. I really need her to help me make some sense of this.*

Not that Nina's hopes of that were particularly high. Unfortunately the scene she'd just seen unfold already made sense—in its own sick, twisted way. It was more a question of learning to believe it than of understanding anything.

Nina reached the second floor and approached

5

Elizabeth's door. Her hand was raised to knock when an unexpected sound made her freeze. Was Elizabeth *crying*? Startled, she bent her head closer to the door, listening. Elizabeth wasn't just crying—she was sobbing her heart out!

"Liz?" Nina called softly. The only answer was an abrupt silence on the other side. "Liz, I'm coming in." Nina rapped lightly, then pushed open the bedroom door, only to find Elizabeth huddled on her bed, her usually pretty face tear-streaked and miserable.

"Elizabeth! What happened?" Nina gasped, rushing over. "Are you all right?"

Elizabeth nodded yes, then shook her head no, then shrugged. "I'm . . . I'm not hurt or anything, if that's what you mean."

"So why are you crying?"

Elizabeth hesitated, then raised her chin. "I . . . I just saw Jessica and Ryan t-together in his room," she stammered, barely able to get it out. "And they . . . they were *kissing!*"

"No!" Nina cried angrily. "I can't believe Jess would do that to you! And what about Ryan? What was his excuse?"

Elizabeth shook her head, her bottom lip twitching. "They never even noticed me," she wailed, bursting into tears again. "They were too busy. . . ."

"Oh, Liz," Nina began, intending to say something comforting, but emotion closed her throat and tears began spilling down her own cheeks. She sank to a sitting position on the edge of Elizabeth's bed. *What an awful, horrible, completely useless night,* she thought. *First Stu and Rachel, and now this.*

"I . . . I guess my bad karma's contagious," she managed at last, trying to smile through her sorrow.

Elizabeth looked up and for the first time seemed to notice that Nina was crying too. "Nina, don't cry! I'm so sorry. I didn't mean to dump all my problems on you."

"I wish my reasons were that noble," Nina admitted with a grimace. "I'm afraid I've been having a little man trouble of my own."

Elizabeth looked confused. "You? With who?"

"Well," Nina admitted slowly, "I kind of met somebody."

"Nina!" Elizabeth exclaimed, sitting up on the bed. "You're seeing someone? After all your speeches about how men are dogs?"

"I *was* seeing someone," Nina corrected. "And incidentally, men really *are* dogs. All of them." Even as she said it, though, she felt her heart wrench inside her chest. Stu had seemed so perfect. So gorgeous. So sweet. So gentle. So different from the others . . .

"Hey, want to hear something weird?" Nina asked, eager to take her mind off Stu's good points. "I ran into Rachel Max tonight."

"Rachel Max!" Elizabeth exclaimed. "From

7

the South Beach Squad? I thought she was in jail for stealing all that money last summer!" Elizabeth was sitting straight up on the bed now, her expression fascinated, her own problems seemingly forgotten.

"She got out," Nina replied. "And she's even more psycho than before. This guy I've been seeing, Stu Kirkwood . . . well, ever since I met him, all this weird stuff's been happening. My bike tire suddenly went flat. Someone tried to push me into hot coals at the beach. Then I found all my bathing suits cut into shreds just before I got knocked unconscious."

Not to mention being lured out into that dangerous surf under the pier to save a plastic doll! she added silently, her face burning with shame at the memory.

"Nina! You should have told me! Why didn't you call the police?"

"And tell them what?" Nina shrugged. "I didn't know *what* was going on. I do now, though," she added grimly. "Rachel Max. She did it all."

"You don't really think that Rachel—"

"Yes, I do. Because now she says she's pregnant with Stu's baby too."

Elizabeth's eyes widened with amazement as she slumped back against her pillow. "His baby?"

"That's what Rachel says," Nina muttered, trying to keep her voice matter-of-fact while inside her emotions raged out of control.

"But is that even . . . uh . . . possible?" Elizabeth asked, blushing slightly.

"Yeah, unfortunately. Stu had a one-night stand with her. That's all."

The very notion of Stu and Rachel together made Nina seethe. Still, Nina had managed to forgive Stu for sleeping with Rachel; after all, it had happened only once, and that was before Nina had even met him. But a *baby!* A baby was something else entirely.

"Wow," Elizabeth said softly. "And I thought *I* had problems. I'm so sorry, Nina."

Nina nodded, grateful for her friend's sympathy.

"What are you going to do?" Elizabeth asked. "It sounds pretty over."

Nina opened her mouth to agree but was amazed to hear herself saying, "I don't know. I thought so when I left his house tonight, but now I'm not so sure."

"But Nina!" Elizabeth protested. "If he got Rachel pregnant—"

"If Stu got Rachel pregnant, it's over," Nina agreed. "But what if he didn't?"

Elizabeth seemed to think about it. "Rachel *is* a liar," she said slowly.

"That's right," Nina said, feeling a glimmer of hope. "A whacked-out, compulsive, psychotic, certifiable liar. And we don't know for sure that Stu's the father. Do you remember how jealous she was when Jessica started seeing

9

Ben last summer? I think she's *twice* as protective of Stu. I'll bet she'd say anything to keep me away from him."

"Probably. But what if he *is* the father, Nina? What will he do?"

"Knowing Stu, he'll marry her," Nina said miserably. "He's too responsible for his own good."

And where does that leave me? Nina couldn't help adding silently. Tears rose up in her eyes again, blurring her vision.

"*Marry* her?" Elizabeth exclaimed, clearly shocked. "Doesn't he know what she's *like*?"

"Yes. But that's how he is, Elizabeth. He knows she's bad, but he won't let it stop him. Stu is the sweetest, most kindhearted, most genuinely good person. . . ." Nina's voice caught on a sob. "Rachel doesn't deserve him."

Elizabeth moved over on the bed and put an arm around Nina's shoulders. "You don't know how things are going to turn out yet," she reminded her friend softly. "Even so, maybe it would be better if you walked away from this one. I know how you feel—*believe* me, I do. But Rachel sounds like even more of a lunatic than she was before. And if this guy Stu is involved with her in any way . . . well, I think you should stay out of it."

"I know. You're right," Nina agreed unhappily. "But I just can't walk away from Stu now. I don't want to."

10

"Nina—"

"Stu is going to talk to Rachel tomorrow night. Alone. After that, if it's his baby, I promise I'll forget I ever knew either one of them."

Elizabeth looked worried. "I just don't want to see you get hurt."

A breathy laugh escaped from Nina's lips. "Too late!" she said lightly, trying to smile through her tears.

"I mean hurt *physically*," Elizabeth corrected, scowling. "She's already attacked you, Nina. And remember last summer when she poisoned Wendy's dog? You have no idea what Rachel will do if you cross her."

Nina sighed. "I know. But even so, I can't just stop loving Stu."

Elizabeth heaved a sigh that mirrored Nina's own. "Tell me about it. When I saw Jessica and Ryan together in his room tonight, I felt like I could kill them both. But if Ryan walked in here right now and asked me to forgive him . . . well . . . I wouldn't be responsible for my actions."

"Some feminists *we* are," Nina joked.

A slight smile crossed Elizabeth's face as she shook her head sadly.

"Well, good night, Liz," Nina said, rising from the edge of her friend's bed. "If we're going to be any good on the beach tomorrow, we'd better try to get some sleep."

11

"Good night," Elizabeth called as Nina shut the bedroom door behind her.

But instead of crossing the hall to her own bedroom, Nina found herself trotting back down the stairs. The light was still on in the kitchen, so Nina pulled a chair over to the counter by the telephone and stood on its wooden seat to reach the high, tiny cupboard where the phone book was kept.

"Let's just see how long old Rachel has been back in town," Nina muttered, climbing down off the chair and thumbing through the phone book. *Max . . . Max . . . bingo!* "Max, Rachel," she read triumphantly. "519C Spindrift Drive."

A slow, thoughtful smile crossed Nina's face. Sure, Rachel knew Nina lived at the beach house, but now Nina knew where Rachel lived too.

Two can play this game, Rachel Max, Nina thought, filled with sudden determination. *If you want to mess with me, you'd better be ready for the consequences!*

"Wow!" Jessica gasped, trying to catch her breath. She couldn't believe that she was finally with Ryan Taylor, but there he was, still lying in her arms on his sofa. *And is he ever worth the wait!* Jessica thought, a satisfied smile on her tingling lips. She let her gaze roam the tan, muscular planes of his body before returning it to settle on his honey-flecked brown eyes.

"Wow, yourself," Ryan said, returning her smile. He bent his head back down to hers and kissed her one last, lingering time before rising from the couch and crossing over to the little sink and counter that served as his kitchen. "Can I get you a drink?" he asked.

Jessica heard the question through a fog. Ryan's skimpy square-cut bathing suit was so sexy, she could barely keep her mind on anything else. She herself had started the evening in a blouse and skirt she'd "borrowed" from Elizabeth, but things had heated up so fast that they'd both needed a moonlight swim to cool down.

"I'd love a diet Coke," Jessica finally managed, self-consciously adjusting a shoulder strap on Elizabeth's sparkling white maillot—also "borrowed." Luckily for Jessica, she had chosen to wear it as a bodysuit under her outfit; the swim would have turned out to be a little *too* risqué without it.

Ryan looked at her strangely, then opened a cabinet and pulled out a liquor bottle. "I don't have any Coke," he said, tipping the bottle over a glass and sloshing out a generous shot. "How about some whiskey?"

Jessica shuddered, imagining the horrid, burning sensation of straight alcohol. "No, thanks."

"Suit yourself," Ryan said with a shrug. *"Salud!"* He raised the half-full glass in her direction, then bolted down the contents in three quick swallows.

Jessica watched in shock, amazed that Elizabeth had never mentioned that Ryan was a drinker. It was almost impossible to picture her judgmental, straight-arrow twin hanging out with someone so cool.

Not that drinking is cool, Jessica quickly reminded herself. She didn't drink herself and usually found it one of the world's biggest turnoffs. *But Ryan totally carries it off. On him it just seems manly . . . sophisticated . . . sexy!*

As Ryan turned back to the counter to pour himself another drink, Jessica left the couch and snuck up behind him, slipping her arms around his bare waist and pressing her face against his muscular back. "You know, I've been waiting for this night for ages," she admitted dreamily. "Ever since the very first time I saw you last summer."

"Oh yeah?" he teased. "That's a surprise. You looked awfully busy with Ben Mercer to me."

Jessica stiffened involuntarily at the sound of Ben's name, then forced herself to relax again. "Ben was nothing to me—just someone to hang out with," she lied, hoping Ryan wouldn't catch on. "*You* were the guy I really wanted."

Ryan put down the whiskey bottle and loosened her arms just enough to turn around and face her. "I like a woman who knows what she wants," he said, flashing a slow, sexy grin. He put his hands on Jessica's shoulders and pulled her tightly against his chest. "I must have been blind

14

to have chosen your sister over you. Elizabeth's a total downer, but you're wild . . . intensely wild."

"Um, I wouldn't call Liz a downer . . . ," Jessica began halfheartedly, knowing she ought to stick up for her sister.

"You're right," Ryan interrupted. "More like a *mega*downer. The two of you are nothing alike." He kissed her lightly. "And that's the way I like it."

Jessica hesitated a moment, then smiled, gratified. *After all, he couldn't be more right,* she told herself. She and Elizabeth *were* nothing alike. Thank heaven Ryan had finally noticed!

"I'm glad you've finally learned to appreciate me," she said, basking in Ryan's compliment. "It took you long enough."

"Well, how about you and I make up for lost time?" Ryan suggested, burying his hands in her long blond hair and kissing her hungrily.

More like make out *for lost time,* Jessica thought dizzily, matching him kiss for kiss. Still, she wished that Ryan hadn't mentioned Elizabeth. The vision of her sister's scolding face kept nagging her.

I'm not doing anything wrong, Jessica reassured herself hastily. *After all, Elizabeth's the dummy who broke up with him. Ryan's a free man. That is, he* was *a free man. Now he's all mine!*

Ryan suddenly broke off the kiss, a devilish gleam in his eye. "I want to propose a toast!" he said.

15

"What?" Jessica replied breathlessly, the taste of Ryan's whiskey lingering in her mouth.

Ryan didn't answer. Instead he grabbed his full glass off the counter and took Jessica by one hand, pulling her out through his front door and onto the Main Tower's outside staircase.

"What are we going upstairs for?" she asked as they climbed in the dark to the wooden observation platform.

"Just come on," he answered mysteriously. "You'll see."

They reached the platform, and the deserted sand spread out beneath them, silver in the moonlight. Jessica breathed in the cool salt air, savoring its smell. "It's so pretty out tonight," she murmured happily.

"Not half as pretty as you are," Ryan returned.

"Mmm. You come here," she said, reaching for him, but he sidestepped her embrace.

"No, I have a toast to make! Wait here."

"What . . . ?" Jessica began, but Ryan was already scaling the tower wall, the glass of whiskey cradled gently in one hand. "Ryan! Be careful!" Jessica called nervously. "What are you doing?"

Ryan pulled himself onto the tower roof easily, the muscles in his broad, bare back and legs flexing tantalizingly with the effort. Mesmerized by his body, Jessica watched as Ryan climbed to the highest point of the roof and grabbed the flagpole with one hand, the glass extended in his other.

"A toast!" he shouted, waving his drink in the direction of the ocean. "Here's to Jessica Wakefield—the most beautiful woman in the world!" Ryan brought the glass to his mouth and slammed back the contents. Then, with terrific strength, he hurled the empty glass far out into the night.

"You're not so bad yourself," Jessica murmured, awed by the sheer romance of the moment. Her heart fluttered wildly and her cheeks felt suddenly hot in spite of the cool night air. She'd never been with anyone so exciting—no, so totally, utterly *perfect*—before.

And here's to you, *Ben Mercer,* Jessica toasted silently as Ryan climbed back down to the platform and swept her into his arms. *In your face, chump!*

"It's about time," Winston Egbert muttered as the gleaming private jet touched down on the local airstrip. He checked his watch nervously, certain they were already way behind schedule, but Pedro Paloma's pilot had timed it perfectly: 8:05 A.M., Thursday morning. The plane rolled smoothly along the runway in Winston's direction.

"Pedro! Pedro! Over here!" Winston yelled frantically before the plane had even stopped taxiing. Several of the other people waiting behind the chain-link fence at the tiny airfield looked at him strangely, but Winston was so happy, he didn't care a bit. He'd actually convinced Pedro Paloma—*the* Pedro Paloma!—to cut short his world tour and fly home from Sweden.

Compared to that, everything else was going to be easy.

He hoped.

"Pedro! Over here, man!" Winston shouted again as the jet door opened and the field attendants began rolling the portable staircase into place. "Ah, what the heck." Ignoring warnings on at least five different signs, Winston burst out from behind the fence and began running across the asphalt toward the plane, unable to contain his relief that Pedro was back in town.

Ever since his friend Wendy Paloma had decided that she wanted to divorce her superstar musician husband and—worse still—that she was in love with *Winston* instead, Winston had felt as if he were walking on eggshells. Sure, he loved Wendy, but not like that!

For one thing, she was married. And even if she weren't, Winston already had a girlfriend, thank you very much. The whole situation was ridiculous. It would have been laughable, actually, if Winston wasn't so afraid that Wendy was about to do something foolish—something she'd regret for the rest of her life.

"Pay-droh!" Winston gasped, reaching the bottom of the gangway and panting for air. The plane had turned out to be farther away from the fence than it had seemed.

"Winston!" Pedro appeared at the top of the stairs, looking tan and rested, the picture of a superstar in his prime. It wasn't until Pedro had descended to the pavement that Winston noticed his light linen suit looked rumpled and slept in, that a day's growth of stubble covered his dark, hollow cheeks, and that the expression in his deep brown eyes was nothing short of haunted. "Tell me this is one of your better practical jokes," he continued, a hopeful half smile on his face, "and I promise not to kill you."

Winston shook his head and pushed a stray brown curl out of his eyes. "I wish it were. Wendy's totally serious, Pedro. You have to do something before it's too late."

"But divorce?" Pedro protested. He waved up the ramp for someone to bring down his luggage and began wandering across the asphalt in the direction of the terminal. "I can understand why Wendy would be feeling a little neglected, but I can't believe she wants to *divorce* me!"

Winston loped along at Pedro's heels. "That's not the worst of it," he said, steeling himself for Pedro's reaction. "I didn't want to say anything over the phone, but I think you ought to know. . . ." Winston took a deep breath. "Wendy, uh, seems to think she's in love with *me* now."

"With *you?*" Pedro spun around to face Winston, his eyes wide and disbelieving. "You'd *better* be kidding me now, Winston, or I *will* kill you."

"It's not like that!" Winston protested quickly. "Nothing's happened! It's just that I'm *there*, that's all. I'm around. And Wendy's lonely."

Pedro stared Winston down for several long moments, but then his gaze softened. "I know," he admitted with a sigh. "But she ought to under-stand that it's not my fault. Ever since the dance remix of 'The Night' took off the way it did, they keep extending my tour. Did I know when I left here that I'd end up in *Sweden*? Of course not!"

"I know you couldn't help what happened with your tour," Winston said reassuringly, keeping up with Pedro's quick pace as he hur-ried around the terminal toward the parking lot. "But you can see why I had to track you down. This whole thing's getting out of control."

"Pedro Paloma!" a startled female voice gasped suddenly from only a few feet away. "I can't believe it! It's *him!*"

"Pedro!" another young woman screamed. "Pedro, I love you!"

Pedro's head jerked up, his eyes scanning the crowd. Women were hustling over from the fence and from the baggage claim area—they were even running out of the terminal to check on the commotion.

"Pedro! Pedro!" The screams spread like wildfire.

"Do exactly as I tell you," Pedro said to Winston, his voice low and clipped. "Are you ready?"

Winston nodded distractedly. Women were beginning to close in from all sides.

"Run," Pedro instructed calmly, then he bolted. Pedro's long black hair and open jacket

21

flapped behind him as he ran, and his scuffed black cowboy boots pounded the pavement in surprisingly fast, fluid strides.

I think he's done this before, Winston realized as he struggled to catch up. Pedro was really flying now, but his crazed female fans were still closing in on them from behind.

"Come *on*, Winston," Pedro yelled back over his shoulder. "If they catch us before we get to the limo, we'll be here for a week!"

"I'm *trying!*" Winston managed, out of breath. He couldn't believe how hard it was to keep up with Pedro. In another few seconds, though, the cramp in his side was going to render him incapable of movement, and it would all be academic anyway.

Panting, Winston glanced behind him at the approaching swarm of beautiful, desirable women. *Why am I even running?* he thought. Suddenly, getting caught by all those gorgeous girls seemed like a notion overflowing with possibilities. After all, they'd already seen him with a major star. Maybe they thought Winston was someone famous too! Winston could just see himself being overtaken by Pedro's admirers—ripping off his shirt, fighting over the scraps, showering him with kisses. . . .

"I can't make it!" Winston gasped to Pedro, halting his steps abruptly. "Save yourself, man. Don't worry about me—I'll try to stall them."

"Oh no, you don't." Pedro's strong hand grabbed Winston by the front of his garish Hawaiian shirt and yanked him forward. "I need you, remember? Now run!"

Winston felt himself being flung roughly ahead of Pedro; only some truly fancy footwork kept him from falling. "Pe*drohhh*," he whined as Pedro pushed him along, one hand planted in the middle of his back. But out of the corner of his eye he could see that Pedro was busy signaling madly to someone across the parking lot. As Winston cleared the curb a black stretch limousine glided in their direction.

"Get in!" Pedro shouted, yanking open the rear door.

"Gladly." Winston tumbled into the cool, dove-gray interior of the limousine, Pedro right behind him.

"Hit it, Andre!" Pedro barked at the driver. "Get us out of here."

"What about your suitcases?" Winston protested.

"Someone will bring them to the hotel later. Let's go!"

The long car screeched out of the parking lot, leaving a crew of screaming, disappointed beauties in its wake.

"Gee, Pedro," Winston teased, his eyes fixed on the steadily shrinking women through the rear window of the limousine. "Tough life. How do you stand it?"

"You have no idea." He sighed, sounding

exhausted and surprisingly serious. "I used to be able to at *least* go out in public. But this last tour has put an end to that completely. I even get recognized in the *men's* room now."

Winston raised his eyebrows.

"Don't ask." Pedro groaned, sinking back into the soft leather seat. "I'm starting to think I'd have been better off staying in Sweet Valley Shore and playing high-school dances for the rest of my life. At least I'd be able to walk the streets—*and* my wife would still love me."

"Wendy still loves you," Winston reassured Pedro earnestly. "She's just really confused right now. That's why you had to come home."

Pedro smiled sadly. "Well, a tour of Sweden isn't worth losing my wife over. But I still don't see why we have to do all this cloak-and-dagger fooling around, Winston. Why can't we just go over to the house and *talk* to Wendy?"

"No!" Winston exclaimed loudly. "I mean, er, that's not a good idea," he said, a little more quietly. "Wendy's really mad at you right now. She thinks she's over you."

Pedro grimaced.

"She's not, of course," Winston added hurriedly. "But we have to make her realize that on her own. This is a very delicate situation—we have to handle it just right."

"And you've got a plan, of course," Pedro said dryly.

"As a matter of fact," Winston admitted modestly, "I do."

"How did I know?" Pedro groaned. He rolled his eyes in mock horror.

"In case you've forgotten," Winston began huffily, "*I'm* the one who got you two together in the first place. I *think* I know what I'm doing."

"I remember. . . ." Pedro trailed off, a faraway look in his eyes. Then he seemed to snap back to the present. "So, OK, Cupid. Let's hear the plan."

Winston smiled, pleased that Pedro was wise enough to see he needed to turn things over to him. "Hey, Andre," Winston shouted, knocking on the limousine's glass divider. "Take us to Pashenka's Costumers on Pendleton Boulevard . . . *toot sweet!*"

Now that I know what she looks like, I ought to be able to spot her, Nina thought distractedly, adjusting the leg elastic on her lifeguard suit as she gazed out over the crowded sand. From Nina's position at the Main Tower railing, the beach lay open and exposed to her view. Even so, Nina felt like the one on display. *She could be watching me from practically anywhere!*

"Where *is* she?" Elizabeth griped suddenly, indignantly. She dropped the binoculars she'd been using to scan the surf zone and turned to face Nina instead.

"Uh, where's who?" Nina blushed, embarrassed

for being so obvious. Somehow Elizabeth must have guessed that she'd been spending her time looking for Rachel instead of concentrating on her job.

"Jessica, of course!" Elizabeth snapped. "Who else?"

"Oh! Um . . . I don't know," Nina stammered. "I have no idea where Jessica is," she added confidently, glad that Elizabeth hadn't caught her after all.

"Well, don't you think you ought to?" Elizabeth asked nastily. "After all, you *are* the head lifeguard now. And you *do* have a squad member who's almost an hour late reporting for work."

"Don't you tell me what I ought to know," Nina said, her voice turning dangerously sharp. She and Elizabeth had been through all this before. The minute things got a little rocky with Ryan, Elizabeth was all over Nina's actions like white on rice. Well, Nina wasn't going to take it anymore. "I'll deal with my squad the way I see fit."

"That's just my point," Elizabeth complained. "You aren't *dealing* with *anything!*"

The beach in front of Nina disappeared behind a blinding curtain of red as she struggled to control her temper. She couldn't let Elizabeth get to her—not this early in the summer, and not over something so trivial. *If I'm going to lead this squad*, Nina reminded herself, *I have to lead by example*. Besides, Nina knew that Elizabeth wasn't really criticizing her leadership skills. She was just begging for reassurance that Jessica wasn't still with Ryan.

"Look. I know what you're going through," Nina said carefully, working to keep her voice calm and reasonable. "But I'm not going to sit back and be a target for your potshots just because Jessica's Jessica. Save it for the person who deserves it."

Elizabeth looked shocked, then seemed to realize the truth in Nina's words. "I'm sorry," she said sheepishly. "I didn't mean to take my problems out on you. But she *is* an hour late, Nina. Where could she be?"

"I have no clue," Nina answered, sincerely hoping the answer didn't lie somewhere in Ryan's Main Tower living quarters. Technically Ryan should have moved out when he relinquished his post, but no one had said anything about it yet. Nina wasn't going to push the issue; she was happier living at the beach house. Still, it wasn't going to be great for morale to have a quitter—not to mention a heartbreaker—constantly in their midst.

"I didn't hear Jess come in last night. Did you?" Elizabeth pressed, her blue-green eyes dark with worry.

"Can't say I did."

"This is unbelievable!" Elizabeth exclaimed. "We don't even know if she came home! I should have checked her room this morning."

"Look, Liz, I know you're upset. But we've

got a job to do here. What do you say we put this stuff out of our minds for now and concentrate on the water?"

Elizabeth looked as if she'd been stabbed through the heart. "That's easy for you to say!" she accused, tossing her blond ponytail indignantly and turning her tan back on Nina. She brought the binoculars back up to her eyes and resumed an obviously halfhearted scan of the surf.

That's what you think, Nina answered silently, painfully aware of her own hypocrisy. Elizabeth Wakefield wasn't the only woman in the world with man troubles—Nina could barely keep her mind on the job herself. *If only Stu would show up and align my chakras or something!* she thought wistfully.

A rapid, furtive movement on the sand suddenly caught Nina's eye, erasing everything else from her mind. She spun in that direction, her heart in her throat.

"Got you!" a towheaded boy shouted, leaping forward and dumping a toy bucket full of salt water all over his teenage sister.

"You little creep!" she screamed, springing to her feet and chasing him down the beach.

Nina's heart thudded up into her throat as she struggled desperately to regain her cool. *It was nothing,* she reassured herself. *Only a kid.*

Only a sneaking, horrible, nasty little kid with hair the exact same color as Rachel Max's,

28

another part of her mind added grimly. Nina still couldn't get used to the idea of the dark, sultry Rachel as a bobbed platinum blonde; then again, very little of what Rachel did made sense at all. Blond she was, and probably wearing baggy clothes and sunglasses. Maybe a hat. Nina resumed her scan of the people on the beach.

Rachel was definitely out there somewhere, watching her. Nina had never been more sure of anything in her life.

"Mmmmmm." Jessica reached her arms overhead, stretching luxuriously in the spacious bed. Sunbeams were filtering through the window, warming her face, and the soft rhythm of the ocean gradually invaded her dreams. She breathed in deeply, savoring the faint scent of coconut oil on the breeze.

What a great day to be alive! she thought. She could hardly wait to go downstairs and rub Ben Mercer's nose in the fact that she was with Ryan now—*really* with him. If she hurried, maybe she could catch Ben in the kitchen before he left for work.

Jessica rolled onto her side and opened her eyes to check the clock radio next to her bed. Instead of the familiar radio, though, her gaze fell on an unfamiliar nightstand and a dingy kitchenette.

"Oops!" she gasped, blinking rapidly. This

wasn't her bedroom—she was still at Ryan's! *We must have fallen asleep,* she realized, sitting up only to find that she was still wearing Elizabeth's white bathing suit. She rubbed distractedly at her eyes and spotted Ryan sleeping on the sofa across the room, facedown in his adorable square-cut bathing suit.

A slow, happy smile crossed her lips. *What a sweetheart,* she thought. She'd been so exhausted the night before that she must have fallen asleep in his arms. Rather than take advantage of the situation, Ryan had carried her from the sofa to the bed, leaving her there to sleep by herself.

I knew you were a gentleman, Ryan Taylor, she told him silently. *I'm sorry I fell asleep last night, but I'll definitely make it up to you tonight!* The promise excited her, making her heartbeat rev up. *If only you were still on the squad, Ryan. Then I wouldn't have to leave you to go to work!*

"Work." Jessica groaned quietly. Oh, well, at least it would give her the perfect opportunity to drop a bunch of hints about Ryan to Ben and his pain-in-the-butt new girlfriend, Priya Rahman. Jessica hated Priya, not even counting the fact that she'd stolen Jessica's ex. The woman was just plain *obnoxious!* Always acting as if she were the only female on the planet who had a brain, always putting on airs and putting Jessica down. Jessica owed that phony suck-up. Owed her big. Her mind wandered for a moment as she tried to imagine the perfect way to exact revenge on Priya, but nothing sweet enough came to mind.

Oh, well, she told herself. *You'll have all day at work to think about it. What time is it anyway?* Rising silently, Jessica began looking for a clock. But when she finally found one, her heart almost stopped.

"Oh no!" she screeched, forgetting that Ryan was still sleeping. "I'm late!" An hour late, to be exact, and she still had to go home and get changed before she could report for work.

"What's the matter?" Ryan asked sleepily from the couch.

"I overslept," Jessica explained tensely, looking around for clothes to put on over her bathing suit. "I'm late for work."

The skirt and filmy blouse she'd worn the night before were nowhere to be seen; with a sinking feeling, Jessica remembered that she'd left them on the beach. Spotting a white polo shirt of Ryan's hanging over the back of a chair, Jessica grabbed it and pulled it on hurriedly over her head. It came to midthigh on her size-six figure. She grunted, satisfied. It would do.

"I have to go," she hissed, pulling on one of her sandals and at the same time hopping over to the couch on her other foot. "Nina's going to *kill* me!" She bent down and dropped a kiss on Ryan's stubbly cheek, kicking over a nearly empty water glass in the process.

"Nooooo. Aw, don't go." Ryan reached up with one hand and clumsily stroked her face, his eyes still closed. "Stay with me."

"Don't be so cute, or you'll break my heart," Jessica told him, smiling. "Anyway, it's only for a while. I'll see you tonight."

"Just stay a few more minutes," Ryan murmured, half asleep.

"Sorry, sweetie," Jessica said, wishing like anything she could. "But duty calls. I'll see you later." Slipping into her other sandal, Jessica headed for the door.

"Later," Ryan called just as she touched the doorknob.

"Later." She stepped outside and closed the door behind her.

Outside, the sun was so bright that Jessica had to squint. Sunlight sparkled off the sand and danced on the waves. The beach was already getting crowded.

"Oh, man." Jessica groaned, fully realizing for the first time how very late for work she was. Nina was going to have kittens!

And that's why you can't let Nina see you, Jessica instructed herself, trying to stay calm. Unfortunately Nina was stationed right over Jessica's head somewhere, probably with Elizabeth as her second. *But they'll be looking at the water,* Jessica reassured herself, *and you're at the back of the station. All you have to do is act casual and head straight for the beach house. No one is going to see you.*

With a quick deep breath for luck, Jessica began striding quickly across the sand in the direction of home. If none of the other lifeguards spotted her, she could get changed and cleaned up and hustle back to Tower 4, where she was supposed to be on duty with her friend Miranda Reese.

Miranda will cover for me, Jessica thought. *And Tower Four is practically on South Beach. No one will know I was more than fifteen minutes late.*

As she hurried away from Ryan's room, though, his scent still warm on the shirt she wore, Jessica couldn't help wishing she didn't have to sneak around unseen. The squad always gathered on the sand next to the Main Tower before everyone took their posts for the day. What a statement it would have made to come swinging out of Ryan's room at the proper moment, all dressed and ready for work! Jessica could imagine snotty Priya's eyes popping as Jessica made her grand appearance, acting as if spending the night with Ryan were the most natural thing in the world.

And Ben! The expression on *his* face would certainly be worth seeing. Oh, sure, he said he loved Priya *now,* but things had been too smooth for him so far this summer. As long as Jessica was available, Ben wasn't going to realize what he'd lost. A little competition would do Ben good!

Oh, well, she told herself. *Things didn't work*

out today. But if I take my clock radio over to Ryan's tonight, there's no reason I can't pull that little stunt tomorrow! She laughed out loud, visualizing everyone's reactions.

And tomorrow is only the beginning, she reminded herself happily. She had all summer to spend with Ryan now. "I can't wait!" she whispered, hugging herself through her new boyfriend's shirt and imagining the thrilling, romantic things they'd do together. "By the end of next week every girl on this beach is going to wish she were me."

Chapter Three

What was that? Elizabeth asked herself, every muscle tensing apprehensively. *Ryan!* The sound she'd just heard coming from the room under the tower had to have been Ryan's front door opening and closing. If only he would come up to the platform and talk to her! There were so many things they needed to discuss.

Elizabeth tried to imagine what she'd say to Ryan if he did come up, and her heart raced painfully. Her feelings were so confused, so raw. When Ryan had started drinking again, at first she'd been worried, then disgusted, then angry. Even when she'd broken up with him, though, she'd known that she still loved him. In the back of her mind she'd secretly hoped that the fear of losing her would make Ryan straighten out. But seeing Ryan kissing Jessica the night before had been one of the ugliest shocks of Elizabeth's life.

I don't know if I even want to talk to him, she thought miserably, feeling like a fool. *Obviously I totally overestimated how much he cares about me. What if he tells me he wishes he'd started out with Jessica in the first place?*

The mere thought made her wince, and a fresh burst of anger surged through her. If Jessica would just stay out of it, then maybe— *maybe*—Elizabeth could put things back together with Ryan. *If that's even what I want now,* she thought with an internal groan. *I don't really know anymore.*

Elizabeth tried to visualize Ryan standing on the platform in front of her. *"Ryan, we need to talk,"* she heard herself saying. No good. It seemed as if she was *always* telling Ryan that they needed to talk. *How about, "Ryan, I can help you stop drinking . . . but only if you stop seeing Jessica"?*

That sounded a lot more to the point. Then again, shouldn't she offer her help no matter what? *I'm a nice person, but I'm not a saint,* Elizabeth thought bitterly, picturing her faithless sister in Ryan's arms again. *And I'm sick of everyone always assuming I'll understand.*

A few moments later Elizabeth had to grudgingly admit to herself that she had no idea *what* she wanted to say to Ryan. She was only sure of one thing: She had to talk to him. If nothing else, she needed to confront him about kissing Jessica. She needed to find out if there was anything left between them. And since he wasn't coming up to her, she'd have to go down to him.

"Cover for me, will you, Nina?" Elizabeth asked quickly. "I need to take a bathroom break."

Nina grunted agreement without looking away from the beach. Her eyes roamed the shoreline distractedly, almost nervously. Elizabeth hesitated a second, then shrugged and raced down the stairs. Nina was in a bad mood today—Elizabeth had already found that out the hard way. And there was no point trying to talk Nina out of anything when she was in one of her moods.

Elizabeth's feet hit the beach at the base of the stairs and were immediately buried in hot sand. Which way had Ryan gone? She scanned the beach in all directions, looking for his tall, broad figure.

He can't have gotten very far, she told herself, puzzled when she didn't see him right away. *He just came out the door!* But there was no one on the beach behind the station who resembled Ryan in the slightest. In fact, the area was all but deserted. The only living thing Elizabeth saw within the proper distance was the back of a briskly walking blond girl who looked a lot like . . .

"Jessica!" Elizabeth exclaimed, furious. Not only did she recognize her twin sister but also the white polo shirt she wore. It was Elizabeth's favorite shirt of Ryan's—the one he'd worn on their very first date. The sight of Jessica strutting around

37

in that shirt was like a sharp slap in the face.

How dare *she spend all night with Ryan, blow off work, and then walk out of there flaunting his clothes!* Elizabeth raged silently, her cheeks flushed with fury. Her entire body trembled as she watched her twin saunter across the sand, clearly very pleased with herself.

Stealing other people's boyfriends always gave her a thrill, Elizabeth thought seethingly, then cringed. *OK, so maybe Ryan isn't* technically *my boyfriend anymore,* she reminded herself. *But that's only technically!* They'd only broken up a couple of days before, and then only because they'd had that horrible fight. Jessica would have to be completely dense not to realize that Elizabeth still had feelings for him.

Instinctively Elizabeth started to run. Jessica Wakefield was about to get told off like she'd never been told off before!

"Jessica!"

Jessica froze at the sound of someone shouting her name behind her on the beach, then relaxed again as she realized who the voice belonged to. It was only Elizabeth. Her sister wouldn't get her in trouble with Nina. On the other hand, Elizabeth might not be the best possible person to run into right now either—especially not if she had any clue where Jessica had spent the night.

That's really none of her business, Jessica reassured herself as she waited for Elizabeth to catch up. *Liz and Ryan were already finished before I got involved with him.*

"Jessica!" Elizabeth stumbled through the final few feet of sand and stopped, glaring at her twin, her hands on her hips.

Uh-oh, Jessica thought uncomfortably. *She does know.* Still, it really *was* none of her business.

"What do you want, Liz?" Jessica asked, her voice impatient. "I'm kind of in a hurry here."

"Yeah. I'll bet you are," Elizabeth sneered nastily. Her cheeks were a brilliant, violent red and her eyes brimmed over with poorly suppressed venom.

"Jeez, what's *your* problem?" Jessica asked, staring at her normally hypercontrolled sister. "You look like you're having a heart attack."

"Just what do you think you're doing?" Elizabeth demanded, ignoring Jessica's question. "I know where you were last night!"

Jessica laughed. "Well, congratulations, Sherlock." She gestured down at Ryan's oversize white polo shirt, then ran a hand through her sleep-tangled hair. "What gave me away?"

"You stay away from Ryan," Elizabeth warned, her blue-green eyes flashing.

"Ex*cuse* me? In case you've forgotten, *you* didn't want him anymore. In fact, you practically handed him to me on a plate," Jessica reminded her sister, starting to feel very much in the right.

"You think you're so smart, don't you?" Elizabeth shouted, all but out of control. "Well, let me tell you something, Jessica—you don't know *anything* about Ryan! Just stay away from him!"

"I will not!" Jessica shot back. "And you can't make me!"

Elizabeth looked ready to explode. She took several deep, shuddering breaths, obviously trying to calm herself. "You have no idea what you're stepping into," she said after a minute, her voice so tight, it shook. "There are things happening with Ryan that you know nothing about."

"So? There are things happening with Ryan that *you* know nothing about." Jessica ran her fingers over the fabric of Ryan's shirt for emphasis.

Elizabeth blanched, then seemed to regain her control. "I'm only saying this because I don't want to see you get hurt, Jessica. Ryan has a . . . big problem. I . . . I can't even discuss it with you. Anyway, you wouldn't understand—"

"Wouldn't understand?" Jessica repeated, enraged. "Don't you *dare* talk down to me, Elizabeth! I am not a child!"

"I *wasn't* talking down!"

"First Priya and Ben start treating me like an idiot, and now you too? Well, let me tell you something. The only 'problem' with Ryan is that he likes me better than you!"

"You don't understand!" Elizabeth protested, tears welling up in her eyes.

"Oh no. I understand *perfectly,* Liz," Jessica accused angrily. "This isn't about me getting hurt, and it isn't about Ryan and his supposed problems. It's all about *you* having second thoughts. Well, too bad! You were an idiot to dump Ryan in the first place, but he's *my* boyfriend now. And you'd better learn to live with it!" She spun furiously on her heel and started running in the direction of the beach house.

"Jessica, wait!" Elizabeth called out behind her.

"Forget it, Liz!" Jessica shot back without turning around. "You and Ryan are history!"

Pashenka Slogodoba put his tiny fists on his delicate hips and stepped back to survey Pedro. "Beautiful!" he pronounced proudly. "Some of my very best work."

"I don't know . . . ," Pedro began hesitantly, tugging at the straggly gray wig that completed his new costume.

"Oh, definitely, Pedro," Winston butted in, casting an anxious glance at the bristling Pashenka. "You look just like that guy on those Curative Essence of Well-being infomercials. Except more, you know, *psychic.*"

Pedro raised two prematurely silvered eyebrows at Winston. "You mean psych-*o.* I look like a deranged Pomeranian trying to pass itself off as Elvis!

Come on, Winston, don't you think this jumpsuit is a little too much?" Pedro gestured down at his gleaming white jumpsuit, flipping the short matching cape off his shoulder in disgust. "And what about this gold medallion? I look like a nut!"

"Enough!" Pashenka exploded angrily. "Never have I been so insulted! You are ungrateful! You do not know fine costuming when you see it!" He stepped forward and plucked the long false mustache mercilessly from Pedro's upper lip. "Fine! Take it off, then. I am finished with you!" He reached for the wig.

"No, Pashenka!" Winston protested, jumping forward and restraining the small, angry man by the shoulders. "We *love* it. Really. If you could just give me a minute alone with my friend . . ."

Pashenka's bottle-green eyes narrowed. "What for?" he asked suspiciously.

"Just give us a minute," Winston repeated urgently. "Please!"

"Very well," Pashenka relented. He directed one last, poisonous look at Pedro, handed Winston the false mustache, and wandered off toward the back of the store.

"Touchy!" Pedro exclaimed as soon as the costumer was out of earshot. "Jeez."

"Well, you *did* make fun of his outfit," Winston said, hoping to restore peace. "The guy's an artist."

"Some artist!" Pedro snorted, examining

42

himself in the full-length mirror. "I still don't see how dressing like a total kook is going to help me win back Wendy."

"Stop fussing with your cape," Winston ordered, ignoring Pedro's skepticism. He held out the false mustache. "And put this back on."

"Ah, Winston," Pedro complained. "Not the mustache! It looks terrible with my beard." Pedro had allowed Pashenka to dye his eyebrows gray but had refused to let the man anywhere near his precisely trimmed goatee. The jet-black whiskers stood out unnaturally now against the faded color of Pedro's wig.

"That's why you have to get rid of the goatee," Winston replied calmly, sticking the false mustache back on Pedro's upper lip. "You can shave it when we get back to the hotel."

"No way!" Pedro exclaimed, his hand flying up to protect his chin. "Not a chance."

"Come on, Pedro," Winston cajoled. "It clashes with the 'stache. And you *need* the 'stache. Besides, the goatee is a dead giveaway. Wendy'll recognize you for sure."

"Oh, *man*." Pedro groaned, wistfully stroking his whiskers.

"I never thought the goatee look was right for you anyway," Winston said soothingly. "Besides, you can always grow another one later."

"But Wendy really likes my goatee!" Pedro protested.

43

Winston's eyebrows shot up involuntarily, but he recovered quickly. Wendy had already confided that she hated Pedro's goatee, but it didn't seem like the best time to tell him so. "You didn't have one last summer, and she married you anyway," Winston pointed out instead.

"I suppose." Pedro held his hand to his chin, considering, then heaved an enormous sigh. "All right. The goatee goes. Anything else, Herr Winston?"

Winston eyed his charge critically. From the wig and mystical gold medallion down to the brass-capped toes of his white, ostrich-skin boots, Pedro looked every bit the part of the quintessential New Age guru. There was just one thing missing.

Moving quickly, Winston stepped over to a nearby counter and selected a pair of enormous black wraparound sunglasses. Then he pushed them firmly onto Pedro's face. "Perfect!" he pronounced.

Pedro turned back to the mirror. "Whatever," he said uncertainly, shrugging his broad shoulders.

"Pashenka!" Winston called, snapping his fingers in the air. "We're ready!"

Pashenka stalked back up to the front of the store, clearly still miffed. He rang up the purchases in silence as Pedro removed his costume.

"So what's next on your agenda?" Pedro

asked Winston, handing over the wig.

"We have to get to work on your hotel suite at the Ocean Palace. We've got a lot of redecorating to do to make the atmosphere just right."

"For what they charge at that place, it ought to come with the atmosphere of your choice," Pedro grumbled. "That atmosphere ought to be able to support alien species!"

"Stop whining," Winston ordered, watching Pashenka wrap each item of the costume in layers and layers of gold tissue paper. "With me on the job, you'll be living at home again in no time."

"So you say," Pedro retorted. "But so far your plan is awfully short on details."

"Look, this is *going* to work," Winston told Pedro as Pashenka rang up the final item. "Tonight we'll get your suite fixed up with candles and crystals, and I'll coach you on exactly what to do. Then tomorrow night I'll bring Wendy over to meet her latest guru!"

"That will be six hundred ninety-two dollars and eighty-four cents," Pashenka announced, a little spitefully.

"Ow!" Pedro exclaimed.

Winston stomped down hard on Pedro's foot. "Uh, he means *'wow!'*" Winston corrected quickly. "What a bargain!"

Pashenka scrutinized them both for a long moment before finally accepting Pedro's credit card. Winston breathed a silent sigh of relief when the costume was paid for and the bags were safely in his hands.

"Thanks for everything!" he told Pashenka, hustling Pedro out to the sidewalk before he could do any further damage.

"Can you believe what that guy charges?" Pedro demanded as he and Winston climbed into the waiting limousine. "I sure hope this works!"

"It will," Winston soothed. *It had better*, he added to himself, starting to feel a little nervous.

Pedro settled grumpily into his seat as Andre pulled out into traffic, but a moment later a smile crept over his features. "That outfit is *bad*, Winston," he said, beginning to laugh. "I'm not sure I can wear it with a straight face."

Winston opened his mouth to protest, but Pedro's laughter was infectious. "It is a little funny, I guess," Winston allowed, chuckling.

"Funny? It's hilarious!" Pedro roared. "Maybe I'll play Vegas. Liberace has nothing on me!"

Winston couldn't resist the image. "And now!" he proclaimed loudly, pretending to be a stage-show emcee. "*Direct* from Sweden, the Las Vegas Hot Spot is pleased to announce The Artist Formerly Known as Pedro Paloma! He's wild, he's live, he's *sassy*, and he's wearing Wayne Newton's clothes!"

Pedro laughed helplessly, tears spilling down his cheeks.

"Ladies and gentlemen!" Winston continued,

encouraged. "Put your hands together for the coolest, the craziest, the most cosmically clad cat around. . . . I give you *Pedrooo Palooomaaa!*"

He gestured grandly at Pedro, then collapsed back into his seat, doubling over at his own wit. Even the normally impassive Andre was cracking up. They laughed that way for nearly a block before Pedro suddenly announced, his voice strangely serious, "This thing with Wendy has got to work, Winston. I'm not kidding."

Winston turned toward his friend. "It's going . . ." He trailed off in midsentence, unsure if the tears in Pedro's eyes were the result of too much laughter or not.

"I don't believe you," Rachel Max said petulantly, twisting the telephone cord while she talked.

"No, Rachel, I really *do* want to see you tonight," her beloved Stuart Kirkwood pleaded on the other end of the line. "I think we need to talk about this. Just the two of us. *Alone.*"

A strange, feline expression crept over Rachel's face. She sat up straighter on the decrepit, squeaking single bed—one of only two pieces of furniture in her pathetic studio at the VistaView Apartments. "I don't think you mean that," she taunted. "I think you're ashamed of me. You and *her*. She wants me to get rid of our baby, doesn't she?"

"Leave Nina out of this," Stuart demanded.

"If you're really having my child, I want to be its father. No matter what. Don't do anything crazy, Rachel."

Rachel smiled triumphantly, her expression reflected in the cracked excuse for a mirror above the battered desk. "I'll think about it," she said.

"Just . . . just come over tonight. I know we can work this out."

Rachel's smile cranked up another notch. "I'm not going to sit around your house talking about something so . . . so *personal* as if it's a problem that needs to be solved." She dropped her voice to a coo. "Don't you remember the night we met, Stuart? How romantic that whole evening was? You wanted me then, didn't you? Oh yes, you *showed* me how much you wanted me."

"Rachel, can we *please* talk about this in person?" Stuart begged.

"Well, *maybe* I could find time to drop by after dinner. . . ."

"I'll *make* you dinner! Just come over."

Rachel gleefully noted how absolutely desperate he sounded. "I knew you'd want me back, Stuart," she purred, falling backward and squirming happily on the unmade bed.

"Yeah. Whatever. Just come over, OK?"

"See you tonight," she said, hanging up the telephone.

The private telephone was the only good thing about Rachel's efficiency apartment in the

48

VistaView complex. Her room was despicable, there was no kitchen, and the bathroom was down the outside hall. But as Rachel stared up at her cracked, grimy ceiling it was another bedroom she saw in her mind's eye—the master bedroom at Stuart Kirkwood's beach-front mansion on SeaMist Island.

"Not much longer now." She chuckled to herself. "Destiny always takes its course."

She'd be with Stuart already, of course, if not for that simpering Nina Harper. "Oh, Stu, you're my *hero!*" she cried suddenly in a sarcastic imitation of Nina. "Let me give you a big, wet kiss!"

A white-hot flash of hatred tore through her, and Rachel shuddered with the sudden violence of the emotion. The way Nina clung to her Stuart, *kissed* her Stuart, was enough to justify whatever actions Rachel had to take to get rid of her.

"You'd better wise up and back off, Nina Harper," Rachel threatened out loud, her voice shaking. "That is, if you want to live to see your next birthday." So far Nina had been luckier than a cat with nine lives, but Rachel was through with indirect methods. If Nina got in her way again, the result was going to be deadly.

Enough! Enough already with that witch Nina! Rachel told herself, sitting back up on the bed. Her hands were shaking with anger, and she felt a vein pounding somewhere in her temple. *Think about something else. Think about Stuart.*

"Yes, Stuart," she repeated, trying to calm her ragged breathing. She breathed in slowly, deeply, the way she'd seen Stuart doing when she spied on his morning meditation. *Now out,* she instructed herself, exhaling fully, imagining herself sitting at Stuart's side in a sexy purple unitard while he meditated. *And I'll do it too,* she vowed. When she was Stuart's wife, she'd be with him everywhere. Every minute of every day.

There, that's better, Rachel soothed herself as her pulse began to slow. *You have to be patient just a little longer.*

Nina was nothing more than a temporary distraction. Rachel would see to that. She rose and walked to the desk, where she studied herself in the mirror, rubbing her stomach in soft, rhythmic circles.

"What I've got here is better than gold," she whispered to her reflection. "Stuart and me . . . and baby makes three."

Chapter Four

"Help! I can't breathe!" Ryan tried to shout, but the towering surf closed over his head, muffling him. Desperately he kicked through the murky green water toward the surface, struggling to see daylight, but the harder he kicked, the farther away the surface got. How could he have been pushed so far under?

I'm going to die, he realized in a rush. *This is it.* His lungs felt as if they were bursting, and blackness filled his head.

Slam! *Slam!*

The sudden noise from the observation platform over his room woke Ryan with a jerk. "Help!" he gasped, still confused by the dream.

Ryan's heart slowed its hammering as he realized that he wasn't drowning. He was smothering himself, sleeping facedown on the couch. He flipped over onto his back with a groan, the pain in his head ferocious. *What idiot is slamming the tower door this early in the morning?* he wondered irately, already certain despite the fog in his brain that his tormentor was none other than Elizabeth Wakefield.

That's exactly the kind of thing she'd do to get me back for quitting the squad and for . . . for everything, he thought, disgusted. Why did she always have to be so predictable? Why did she always have to be such a drag?

Ryan sat up on the couch and groaned as the room whirled dizzily around him. What a hangover! Was it his imagination, or were they getting worse? He dropped his shaggy head into his hands and whimpered with the pain, stopping a second later when he realized how pathetic he must look.

"So you're a little hung over," he muttered angrily. "So what? A couple of shots will fix you right up." But he didn't move from the sofa.

Then, in an unexpected flash of intuition, Ryan saw what his entire day would be like.

He'd have a drink or two to get going. After that he'd feel better, so he'd have another one. By noon he'd be craving a bender. Then the drinking would start in earnest. By five or six P.M. he'd be tipsy, by seven he'd be drunk, and by nine he'd be blotto. Sometime around midnight he'd pass out. *And tomorrow I'll start the whole thing over again,* Ryan thought, chilled by the sudden clarity of his vision.

"What are you *doing?*" He groaned suddenly, squeezing his temples between his hands. "You have to stop!"

Ryan's head throbbed in response, and his stomach felt strangely hollow. Every nerve ending in his body begged for a numbing dose of alcohol.

"Breakfast and some aspirin. *That's* what you need," Ryan told himself, determined to fight the craving. But for the first time since he'd started drinking again, Ryan was afraid. *It's got you bad this time,* a voice in his head warned. *What if it won't let you quit?*

"That's ridiculous," he answered sharply. "I did it before. I can quit anytime."

Then quit now, the voice argued. *Do it today, while you still can.*

Unsettled, Ryan lurched to his feet and stumbled toward the kitchenette. Halfway there he tripped over a stray glass, launching a cascade of lukewarm liquid over his foot and soaking the carpeting.

"Damn!" he cursed, bending to retrieve the glass. He sniffed at it cautiously as he walked to the kitchen sink. "Just water," he grunted, relieved. Jessica must have left it there.

Oh yeah. Jessica.

Ryan turned back around to examine his room. He'd completely forgotten that Jessica had come over the night before, but he saw now that she'd left his bed in a mess. The covers were half off, the sheets were impossibly twisted, and a pair of silver hoop earrings lay forgotten on the nightstand. *I'll bet Elizabeth would have made that bed with hospital corners,* Ryan couldn't help thinking as he turned back toward the kitchenette. Oh, well. At least Jessica didn't nag him.

He dropped the glass in his hand into the metal sink, regretting it instantly. *Big mistake,* he thought as the harsh, clanging sound reverberated through his head. *Now where did I put those aspirin?* Ryan searched the utility cabinet, then rifled through a couple of drawers. Nothing. His breathing was coming in increasingly shallow, nauseated gasps, and his head was on fire. If he didn't sit down in a minute, he'd puke.

"Where are those stupid aspirin?" he shouted, frustrated. He peered into the very back of the cabinet again, and his eyes landed on an unexpected treasure—a full bottle of whiskey he'd hidden away. Ryan sucked his breath in sharply. Just what he needed!

You'd be better off with the aspirin, man, the voice in his head advised.

"But I can't *find* the damn aspirin!" he shouted angrily, reaching for the liquor bottle. The clear amber liquid sparkled and beckoned in the stray rays of sunlight filtering through the blinds. Ryan turned the bottle over and over in his hands, inspecting the label, running his fingers over the raised lettering under the heel, testing the seal on the cap. It was perfect. Perfect in every way. He wandered back to the couch in a trance and dropped onto the tweed cushions, the bottle still in his hands.

You are *drowning*, the voice insisted. And maybe it was true. Last summer his world had looked so different. He'd been strong then, in control of his drinking and his life. Things at A.A. had been going great. Patti had been there for him. Elizabeth had been there for him.

"Yeah, but where are they now?" Ryan snorted, suddenly wondering what time it was. He dug his diver's watch out of the couch cushions and strapped it onto his wrist. It was after two o'clock. He groaned, disgusted with himself for sleeping so late again.

Not that I have any reason to get up anymore.

"No reason at all," he reassured himself bitterly. "In fact, according to my own thrilling itinerary, the only thing I have to do today is get good and drunk." He popped the seal on the bottle of whiskey and brought it up to his mouth, gulping down as much of the searing liquid as he could without gagging. "And I'm already way behind schedule."

"Last night was *so* amazing." Jessica sighed dreamily, glancing up at Miranda Reese over the top of her sunglasses. "Ryan is such a romantic."

Miranda smiled good-naturedly from her position

55

at the rail of Tower 4. "Somehow I never really thought of Ryan as the romantic type," she said, her wide brown eyes amused.

"I know!" Jessica agreed. "But he's totally changed since he broke up with Elizabeth. We laughed and danced and had the greatest time. And oh, Miranda, the way he *kisses!*" Jessica added, feeling her knees go slightly weak. "He does the cutest little thing with his mouth—"

"Spare me the details," Miranda interrupted, laughing, "or I'll never be able to look the guy in the face again." She shook her head, her straight brown ponytail switching between the red bathing suit straps extending over her strong, tan shoulders.

"It was just so *incredible*," Jessica enthused. "Like it was meant to be. I can't believe we wasted all last summer with other people!"

"Speaking of other people, isn't Elizabeth going to be pretty upset about this?" Miranda asked.

Jessica felt the light of her enthusiasm dim just the tiniest bit. "Elizabeth has no right to be mad at me," she said crossly, remembering the angry words she'd exchanged with her twin that very morning. "If anything, I should be mad at her!"

"What for?"

"For acting like a total wacko! Liz didn't want him anymore—she made that loud and clear. And now she's mad at me because I *do!* Well, I'm sorry, but Elizabeth is an idiot if she thought a hunk like Ryan Taylor was going to languish around on his own for more than a day and a half."

"Oh, my. Was it a whole day and a half?" Miranda asked innocently, the corners of her full mouth twitching toward her dimples.

Jessica smiled in spite of herself. "Well, I had to wash my hair before I went over there. But really, Miranda," she added seriously. "You should have heard Elizabeth carrying on this morning, like I was the biggest backstabber in the world. Not only that, but she practically told me to my face that I wasn't *smart* enough to date Ryan!"

"Not *smart* enough?" Miranda repeated, her expression shocked.

"I know! Like dating guys is brain surgery or something! She kept going on and on about how I didn't know what I was getting into and how I'd wind up getting hurt."

"But why does she think you'll get hurt?"

Jessica shrugged, then smiled smugly as an answer occurred to her. "Personal experience, I guess. But that was *her* fault! She's just jealous."

"Wow," said Miranda, shaking her head. "I don't know her that well, but I really didn't think Elizabeth was like that."

She's not, a tiny voice in the back of Jessica's head piped up, but she ignored it. What else would explain that completely unnecessary scene on the beach this morning?

"Oh, great," Miranda said suddenly under her breath, changing the subject. "Don't look now, but here come Ben Hur and Priya the Terrible."

"More like Ben *Hers*," Jessica grumbled, following her friend's gaze out to the water's edge. Ben was carrying a trash-patrol garbage bag while Priya simpered along at his side with the collection stick. "Oh yeah, they're getting a lot done," Jessica added through gritted teeth as Priya pranced in front of Ben, kicking sea foam at his chest.

As usual, Priya looked exotic and beautiful, her long, glossy black hair swinging.

As usual, Ben looked completely besotted.

"Oooh, I *hate* that snotty witch!" Jessica couldn't help exclaiming.

"*You* hate her," Miranda rejoined, squinting evilly in the direction of her stuck-up roommate. "You don't have to *live* with her!"

"I might as well, the way those two are always hanging out at the Krebbs place." Jessica felt her blood pressure rising; it always did when she saw Ben at the side of that phony. "Well, I certainly moved up to first class when I traded Ben in for Ryan," she said with forced lightness. "Compared to Ryan, Ben's about as handsome as that stuff he's picking up."

Miranda giggled appreciatively. "You know who's hot?" she volunteered, pointing down the beach in the opposite direction. "Theo."

Jessica turned her head and spotted Theo Moore's tall, muscular shape against the water's edge. His red lifeguard trunks stood out like neon against the perfect dark cocoa of his skin, and his safety whistle dangled above the most chiseled abs Jessica had ever seen. "He *is* kind of cute," she allowed distractedly, her mind still on Ryan. "Do you like him?"

"No! He's my housemate! I thought that maybe *you*—"

"Miranda!" Jessica protested, shocked. "You know I'm dating Ryan."

"I know." Miranda winked. "Just something to keep in mind."

"You're terrible!" Jessica told her, laughing. "One boyfriend is plenty, thanks."

"Yeah? Well, don't look now," Miranda said with a smile, "but here comes your Romeo at three o'clock!"

Jessica peered down from the tower to see Ryan crossing the beach to her right, wearing long surfer shorts and a striped T-shirt. His wavy brown hair looked slightly damp, as if he'd just showered. Ryan strode through the sand with his head held high, everything about his tall frame exuding strength and confidence.

"What a babe," Jessica said under her breath, not even aware she was speaking out loud.

Miranda laughed. "Go say hi," she urged.

Not hesitating a second, Jessica raced down

the tower stairs and hurried across the sand toward Ryan. When he removed his sunglasses, the sunshine in his brown eyes picked up their golden highlights.

"Hey, beautiful," he said, his sexy grin widening.

For a moment Jessica was almost too dazzled to return his greeting. "Hey, yourself!" she managed, pulling herself together. "What brings you all the way down here?"

Ryan shrugged and smiled flirtatiously. "Could be I needed the exercise. Could be I needed a kiss."

Jessica raised one perfectly sculpted eyebrow. "And you thought you'd find someone to kiss you down here?" she teased.

"Well, I *hoped* I would. But if you don't want to . . ." Ryan turned around, as if to walk away.

"No! Don't go!" Jessica giggled, jumping up onto his back for an impromptu piggyback ride. Ryan barely stumbled as her unexpected weight settled onto his back. He regained his balance easily and trotted down the beach, bouncing Jessica wildly.

"Ryan!" Jessica squealed with delight, her bare legs dangling. "Ryan, stop!"

"I thought you wanted a ride." He picked up the pace, making Jessica bounce even harder.

"I did, but you're going too far! I have to get back to the tower."

Ryan slowed down and gradually lowered Jessica

back onto her feet. "Blow off the rest of your shift," he urged. "Come have an early dinner with me."

"You know I can't do that!" she protested, surprised. "Besides, there's only another hour left. Why don't I come over to your place after I get showered? We'll go to dinner then."

"I don't know," Ryan said slowly, a mischievous glint in his eyes. "I might find another girl who wants to go out with me before that."

"Ryan!" Jessica giggled, slapping playfully at his arm.

Moving quickly, Ryan intercepted her blow, catching her lightly by the wrist and pulling her hard against his chest. "How about that kiss?" he breathed.

Jessica kissed him as if in a dream, barely aware of the people all around them on the beach. Ryan tasted wonderful—fresh and minty. The kiss went on and on.

"Mmmm," Ryan said after a minute. "*That's* what I needed."

Jessica opened her eyes to gaze into his, but a movement over Ryan's left shoulder caught her attention instead. It was Ben, staring at her openly, a totally unreadable expression on his flushed face. A deliciously evil impulse made Jessica raise one hand slightly and wave.

Immediately Ben spun away from her. The motion caused his bulging trash bag to rip, the garbage spilling all over the beach.

"Ben!" Priya's earsplitting falsetto wailed. "What are you *doing?*" She looked up the beach in Jessica's direction as Ben dropped to his knees to recover the trash.

Jessica wiggled her fingers again in triumph.

"Ben!" Priya repeated, alarmed. Ignoring the scattered garbage, she grabbed her stunned boyfriend by the arm and started dragging him down the beach, staring poisonously at Jessica the entire time.

Jessica savored the sight a few moments longer, then closed her eyes lazily, blocking out the pleasant scene as she kissed Ryan one last, lingering time.

"I don't know what's gotten into Jessica," Nina said darkly, looking down the beach. Even though it was a little past five o'clock and Jessica was officially off duty, it was bad news to be carrying on the way she was while still in her red lifeguard suit. The people on the beach would never know that Jessica wasn't on duty. She'd make the entire squad look bad!

Elizabeth turned to glance in the same direction, then whirled quickly away after she'd obviously caught a glimpse of Jessica and Ryan walking up from Tower 4 with their arms around each another, totally into themselves. Nina watched in angry silence until they started kissing on the sand a short distance from the tower.

"Oh, that's it," Nina snapped. "First she's

over an hour late, and now *this*. Jess had better start taking this job seriously if she wants to keep it. You can tell her I said so."

Elizabeth turned slowly back toward the scene and winced visibly. "You . . . *you* should talk to her, Nina," Elizabeth said, her voice shaky. "Tell her she needs to shape up."

Nina could see that Elizabeth was barely holding back tears, and she felt a sudden stab of sympathy. "It hurts, seeing them together like that," she guessed, putting a hand on Elizabeth's arm.

Elizabeth's eyes brimmed over. "Don't," she warned, her voice strangled. "Don't, or you'll make me cry."

Nina nodded and dropped her hand. It had to be tough for Elizabeth to have had her relationship yanked out from under her so suddenly. Not to mention the way Jessica was rubbing her nose in it at every opportunity. "What I don't get is how Jess can treat you this way. She must know it's killing you."

Elizabeth shook her head. "She thinks she's totally in the right. I told her that Ryan and I were finished, but . . . but I didn't really mean it. Not the way *she* thinks. Anyway, she's not thinking about anyone but herself right now. I know how Jessica is when she gets like this."

"Like what?"

"Desperate for attention," Elizabeth explained. "Right now her self-image is in the gutter. Ben

63

and Priya dumped all over her, so Jess thinks she'll make everything better by throwing herself at Ryan. You know, like, 'Wow, someone likes me again—problem solved.'"

"You really think that's it?" Nina asked skeptically. "After all, Jessica *has* had her eye on Ryan for a long time."

"I *know* that's it," Elizabeth replied grimly. "I tried to tell her what she was getting into, and she wouldn't listen to a word I said."

"What do you mean, 'what she's getting into'?" Nina repeated, confused. "You mean between you and her?"

"No! I mean between her and Ryan. Ryan isn't what you think, Nina. He has some secrets that aren't very nice."

Nina was surprised to hear Elizabeth speak so negatively, but after a second she shrugged. "I always thought that mysterious, brooding thing kind of worked for Ryan. And anyway, I thought *you* were in love with the guy."

"He's an alcoholic, Nina," Elizabeth said quietly, suddenly, her eyes begging Nina to understand, to help somehow.

"He's what?" Nina exclaimed, outraged. "For how long?"

"I don't know, but he's been sober for the last couple of years. That is, he *was* sober—until last weekend," Elizabeth said miserably. "Now he's drinking again."

A confused mix of emotions tore through Nina. She felt disgusted, angry, betrayed. The blood rushed poundingly to her dark cheeks, and her breathing grew short and shallow. Everything about Ryan made perfect sense now: his long absences from work her first summer at Sweet Valley Shore, the working tensions of the summer before, and, most of all, his self-indulgent, incredibly irresponsible behavior so far this season.

"I can't believe him!" Nina shouted furiously. "He *completely* let us down. The squad's short a lifeguard, I'm stuck with a position I never wanted, and . . . for *what*? So Ryan can drink himself to death? It's sickening!"

"Try to understand," Elizabeth begged. "He's been so strong for so long. You know how Ryan is when he's sober—no one cares about this squad more than he does. But he's sick now, Nina. He needs our help."

Elizabeth looked so concerned, so earnest, that Nina relented slightly. "Well, if he needs our help, then I think we ought to confront him. Maybe we should get the squad together for one of those interventions."

"No!" Elizabeth protested, her aqua eyes wide and horrified. "It would kill him to have everyone know his secret, Nina. You know Ryan's pride. An intervention would only drive him further away."

"Then what do you suggest?" Nina returned

impatiently. "If we're not allowed to talk to the guy, and we don't 'officially' know there's a problem, how are we supposed to help him?"

"I don't know," Elizabeth admitted, turning her head away as the tears began spilling down her cheeks.

"Listen, the shift's over," Nina said softly. "I can lock up by myself. Why don't you get out of here?"

Elizabeth nodded gratefully, pausing only long enough to grab her jacket before hurrying down the stairs. Nina remained at the rail, her eyes on Ryan and Jessica.

So Ryan Taylor, Mr. Perfect Lifeguard, is an alcoholic, Nina thought, still trying to digest that amazing information. *Well, it looks like Ryan's past is catching up with him now. Just like Stu—*

Nina winced, cutting off the thought. But she couldn't keep Rachel Max's psychotically twitching face from filling her mind's eye. With an effort Nina replaced Rachel's twisted image with Stu's sweet, patient one. Stu Kirkwood was everything Nina had ever imagined in a guy. After everything they'd overcome to be together—after putting that one-night stand behind them—it hurt more than Nina would have thought possible to be on the verge of losing him.

I guess the past catches up with everyone . . . sooner or later, she thought, tears burning her dark eyes.

Chapter Five

"OK! We'll put the gong over here, the incense over there, and the aromatherapy diffuser in the corner, and we'll light candles all along that wall," Winston announced, beaming as his New Age vision took shape before his eyes.

"Groovy," Pedro responded sarcastically.

"The problem with you is you have no imagination," Winston returned, unruffled.

A full afternoon of strenuous shopping had yielded the raw materials for Winston's master plan, and now, as the sun set spectacularly over the beach outside Pedro's hotel suite windows, Winston worked on the finishing touches. Already the walls of the spacious living room had been draped with yards and yards of a pale watered silk that iridescently reflected all the colors of the setting sun.

"Everyone does black," Winston had explained

while Pedro had paid for the outrageously expensive bolt of fabric. "We're going for a white-light, harmonious-energy kind of look."

"If you say so," Pedro had replied, rolling his eyes.

Now, looking at the way that three of the living room walls shimmered with pale, shifting colors, Winston knew he had made the right choice. On the fourth wall the open French doors framed the ocean, practically bringing it into the room. Winston dragged the antiqued gong into position by himself and began setting up the boxloads of white pillar candles they had purchased earlier. "You want to give me a hand with these?" he asked Pedro.

With a groan Pedro rose from the one comfortable chair left in the room and joined Winston, who was on his knees, arranging candles. "Where do you get your energy?" Pedro asked, dropping down cross-legged beside him. "I'm still exhausted from moving all that furniture!"

Winston grinned. "You have to admit it was worth the effort. The place looks great."

At Winston's insistence the two men had crammed most of the pastel pink and mint green furniture from the living room into the bedroom, leaving only an enormous high-backed chair for the "Master," a small Queen Anne for his "disciple," and a low, square glass table. The Master's chair was centered on the plush cream-colored carpeting, its back to the ocean. The glass table and the smaller chair sat in front of it, facing back toward the French doors.

"This is perfect!" Winston had enthused while he and Pedro had arranged the furniture. "Wendy will be looking into the sunset, and that will make it hard for her to see your face. Meanwhile you'll be able to see every little detail of hers."

"I can't see *that* soon enough," Pedro had replied wistfully at the time. Now all he said was, "I hope this little plan of yours works."

Winston shoved a candle into a black wrought iron holder. "It *will,*" he said reassuringly. Now that he saw how beautifully the whole suite had turned out, he was totally sure of it. "You just need to relax, man. Everything's going to be fine."

"I still don't like the idea of fooling Wendy," Pedro said, his dark eyes troubled beneath their ridiculous silver brows.

"We're not going to fool *anybody* if you don't shave off that goatee like I told you to," Winston replied.

Pedro's hand flew up to his chin protectively. "Ah, come on, Winston. Are you *positive* that's necessary?"

"Yes! Now just do it," Winston ordered. "Do it for Wendy."

"Well, all right," Pedro agreed, his expression softening. "For Wendy."

"You really love her, don't you?"

"Of course," Pedro said fervently. "More than she knows."

"Then stop worrying," Winston directed. "Trust me, this is going to be a cinch. The way I've been running Wendy through the psychic gauntlet the last few days, she's willing to believe anything."

"But I don't want to deceive her!" Pedro protested. "I don't want to prey on her vulnerability."

Winston took a second to consider. "Look, you love Wendy, right?"

"I just said I did."

"And this is your chance to tell her! All you have to do is pretend you're a guru and that you're psychically channeling everything Wendy tells you to Pedro. Then you tell her what Pedro says back. What harm can there be in that?"

"It isn't honest."

Winston put his hands to his head and tugged his own curls in frustration. "Well, it isn't *lying*. It's just . . . uh . . . creative truth telling. Try to go with the flow a little, Pedro."

"It's just that this is so *important!*" Pedro exclaimed, jumping up off the floor and pacing nervously. "Do you realize what you're playing around with here, Winston? Wendy is my *life!* There's nothing I care about more than our marriage."

Winston gulped. When Pedro put it that way, it *did* seem pretty risky. Still . . .

"It's not like you're out on this limb by yourself, Pedro," Winston reminded him. "I have a girl-friend, remember? If Wendy hasn't decided she's not in love with me by the end of the summer, *you* can explain the problem to Denise Waters."

"There she is," Elizabeth said under her breath. From the window of her second-story bedroom Elizabeth had just spotted her twin crossing the lawn in front of the beach house. Thankfully Ryan wasn't with her.

"OK, now," Elizabeth whispered, psyching herself up. "If you want Jess to listen to you, you're going to have to stay calm. As long as she thinks you're jealous, you won't get anywhere with her."

Only a short while earlier, when Elizabeth had fled the Main Tower in tears, she'd been so upset that she couldn't have imagined speaking to Jessica ever again. But now she knew she had to try. No matter how much it hurt her, no matter how painful it was to see Jessica with Ryan, there was too much at stake to sit back and wait for the consequences.

"I just wish she'd listened to me this morning!" Elizabeth moaned. She couldn't think of anything she wanted to do less than discuss Ryan's drinking problem with her sister, but Elizabeth knew now that she'd gone about things all wrong before. She really *was* jealous. And of course that jealousy had come screaming through when she'd flown off the handle.

71

You have to stay calm this time, Elizabeth cautioned herself. *You have to make Jessica understand that this isn't about who "gets" Ryan. It's about making sure he gets help.*

Besides, as vulnerable as Jessica was this summer, Ryan really *could* end up hurting her badly. Not to mention that when he was drunk, Ryan was a physical danger to himself and everyone around him. *What if they get in some kind of accident?* Elizabeth wondered, her stomach hollow with dread as she imagined the possibilities.

The sound of bare feet echoed suddenly on the landing outside Elizabeth's door as Jessica flew by on her way upstairs. Elizabeth immediately snapped out of her thoughts, wanting to catch her twin before she could leave again. With a quick, deep breath to gather her courage, Elizabeth climbed the stairs to Jessica's attic room.

"Jessica?" Elizabeth called, knocking on the frame of Jessica's open door. "Can I come in?"

Jessica was standing in front of her closet, picking out an outfit. At the sight of Elizabeth her aquamarine eyes narrowed suspiciously. "What for?" she asked rudely. "I'm getting ready to take a shower."

"Oh. Are you going somewhere?" Elizabeth asked, desperately hoping her question sounded casual.

"I have a date with Ryan," Jessica told her. "*Not* that it's any of your business. And I don't have time for more of your lectures tonight, Liz, so if you'll kindly get out of my way . . ." Jessica walked toward the open door, her makeup kit in one hand and a terry cloth robe in the other.

"This will only take a minute, Jessica," Elizabeth pleaded. "Please, just listen to what I have to say."

"I heard what you had to say this morning," Jessica retorted. "And it wasn't very nice. I'm not a baby, Elizabeth. I can take care of myself."

"I know you can, Jess. But this isn't a normal situation. You don't know what you're getting into."

"If you say that one more time, I'll scream!" Jessica snapped, her blue-green eyes flashing. "'You don't know what you're getting into,'" she mocked in a priggish, stuck-up voice. "'Only I, the great Elizabeth, am intelligent enough to date Ryan Taylor!'"

Elizabeth felt her own eyes widen. Was that what Jessica believed? That Elizabeth thought her sister wasn't *smart* enough to handle Ryan?

"Listen, Jess. This has nothing to do with intelligence, OK? It's just that . . . that . . ." She took a deep breath and plunged recklessly ahead. "Ryan has a drinking problem, all right? I didn't want to tell you because he doesn't want anyone to know. But I swear it's the truth. And I'm worried about you. I'm worried about *both* of you. Ryan needs help now, not good times."

Jessica stared at Elizabeth, clearly amazed,

and for a moment Elizabeth thought she'd finally gotten through. Then Jessica tossed back her head and laughed.

"The things you'll stoop to!" she said scornfully. "Maybe you're insane with jealousy, or maybe you're just plain insane. Either way I thought you had a little more dignity, Liz."

Elizabeth bristled. "What do you mean?"

"It's over, Elizabeth. No amount of lying on your part is going to change that."

Jessica tried to push past Elizabeth and out the door, but Elizabeth grabbed her sister's arm, furious. "I'm not lying!" she cried. "How dare you say I am?"

Jessica shook off Elizabeth's hand in one quick jerk. "Because it's so obvious! You just can't stand it that he's with me now. Ryan has no more of a drinking problem than you do!"

"You don't know—"

"Last night was the most romantic night of my life," Jessica interrupted. "Ryan was a dream. We danced for hours, went swimming in the moonlight, and then . . . oh yeah. He had a *drink!* In fact, he poured himself a whiskey right in front of me. Then he climbed onto the roof of the Main Tower with it, yelled down to the entire beach that I was the most beautiful woman in the world, and drank a toast to me. *Me!* If that's your idea of a problem," Jessica added sarcastically, "then I can't wait to see it develop into a crisis."

Elizabeth stood aside, dumbfounded, as Jessica glided haughtily from the room. *Ryan never did* anything *like that when he was dating me,* she thought, her surroundings blurring from a sudden rush of tears. *He never even wanted to hold my hand in public!*

Elizabeth tried desperately to imagine Ryan climbing to the tower roof to toast her beauty to the entire world, but the image wouldn't come. It was just so unlike the Ryan she knew.

Well, of course it is, she told herself miserably as she ran back down the stairs and threw herself, sobbing, onto her cold twin bed. *Ryan was sober when he was dating* me.

But the thought didn't make her any happier.

Rachel put down the mascara brush and checked her reflection carefully. Her light brown, almond-shaped eyes were heavily made up, but the lipstick on her pouty mouth was pale. It was an interesting effect. Rachel liked how it looked with her platinum blond hair.

Not that she planned to be a blonde much longer. In fact, she could change back to her normal dark brown color and start growing her hair long again anytime she wanted to now. There was no need to hide anymore.

"That's right. We're coming out of the shadows. And tonight is just the beginning—the beginning of everything I've been waiting for,"

Rachel breathed, admiring herself in the cracked mirror. The sight of the outfit she was wearing shocked her momentarily, but then a slow, satisfied smile crept onto her pale lips.

"I *was* getting sick of those baggy housecoats," she murmured, turning to view herself from all angles. It was a good thing she'd saved her favorite pair of jeans when she'd sold off the rest of her clothes for cash. The worn blue denim hugged her like a second skin, emphasizing every curve. And to top off the jeans, Rachel had liberated a sexy red crop top from the clothesline of a certain Victorian beach house.

Probably Jessica's, Rachel thought with distaste, wishing it could have been Nina's. But Rachel couldn't take a chance on Stuart recognizing the blouse and getting all bent out of shape. She preened in front of the mirror, sucking in her already flat stomach. Soon the baby would begin to show and tight clothes like the ones she was wearing would have to be put away for a while.

Rachel couldn't wait. *What man can resist the sight of a woman pregnant with his child?* she asked herself triumphantly. She'd happily wear maternity smocks for the rest of her life if it meant hanging on to Stuart. Smirking, Rachel sauntered to the window overlooking the back alley and drew her curtains wide.

The grimy window was already open a crack, but Rachel heaved at the decaying wooden sash until it was up as far as it could go. A cool evening breeze rushed into the apartment, carrying the scents of salt air, garbage, and night-blooming jasmine. Rachel breathed in deeply in spite of the garbage smell as she stared out her second-story window into the darkness.

She couldn't see it, but she knew Stuart's private island lay out there in the night. She turned her face in its direction and projected her thoughts toward him. *Soon, my love,* she told him telepathically. *Very soon.*

Now, in fact. Why wait any longer? Leaving the window open, Rachel grabbed her car keys off the scarred, dirt-encrusted top of her desk. A moment later she was outside on her front door landing, locking the dead bolt. Then, with a shiver of excitement, she hurried down the cracked concrete stairs to street level.

Her Taurus was parked in its assigned parking space in front of the building. Rachel climbed into it hurriedly and turned the key in the ignition. The beat-up old car coughed reluctantly to life, and Rachel checked the gas gauge. There was barely enough gasoline for a one-way trip. If she didn't fill up the tank in town before she left, she was sure to run out and be stranded on the island.

Perfect, she thought, smiling broadly. *Stuart may not know it yet, but one way is as far as I intend to go.*

*　　　*　　　*

"Bye-bye and good riddance," Nina said, stepping out from the bushes across the street as Rachel's dirt-brown Taurus disappeared around the corner.

Nina stopped to brush some yellow acacia fluff off her bare arms before locking her bicycle to one of the shrubs she'd been hiding behind. Satisfied that her bike was safe and well hidden, Nina crossed the street toward the ugly, two-story apartment building Rachel had so recently exited.

She just had *to live on the second floor,* Nina complained silently as she crept nervously up the stairs. She felt incredibly exposed and conspicuous, as if at any moment someone was going to realize she was an intruder and start hollering for the police. Her heart in her throat, Nina sidled up to the door she'd just seen Rachel come out of and tried the knob. *Locked.* Squelching a groan of disappointment, she moved over a couple of feet, put both hands on the front window, and pushed. *Also locked.* Now what?

Quickly, before anyone could notice her, Nina trotted back down the stairs. *Maybe there's another way in,* she thought hopefully, even though it didn't seem too likely. Still, Nina had to try. She quickly skirted the end of the apartment building and moved into the alley, counting off back windows until she came to Rachel's.

"Bingo," Nina breathed at the sight that met her eyes. Rachel's single back window was wide open, the shabby, stained curtains billowing in the evening breeze.

It was dark in the alley, and Nina sank back into the shadows, considering her strategy. A huge, foul-smelling Dumpster lay almost directly under Rachel's window. Even so, it wasn't tall enough to boost Nina to the second story.

Inspired, Nina ran along the alley, checking each Dumpster at the adjacent apartment buildings. At the third one she found the treasure she'd been searching for—an old, discarded wooden chair. Pouncing, Nina grabbed it and hurried back down the alley to Rachel's window. A moment later the chair was balanced on top of the Dumpster and Nina was teetering precariously on top of her makeshift ladder.

She reached cautiously for Rachel's windowsill, her hands straining to touch the rough, splintered wood. Her fingers brushed against it, but it was too high. There was no way she'd be able to get a good grip and pull herself into the window from so far below it.

Slowly, carefully, Nina lifted one foot and placed it on top of the narrow chair back. The chair wobbled wildly, and Nina grabbed frantically at the decaying windowsill, squeezing until her knuckles hurt. With an effort she managed to regain her balance. Then, holding her breath so as not to make a single extra movement, Nina brought her second foot up to her first and gradually, deliberately straightened her legs.

"I'm in!" she whispered triumphantly as her head came up even with the bottom of the window. From here it would be a cinch. Pushing off slightly from the chair, Nina hoisted herself up into the window as far as her abdomen.

Crash!

The wooden chair tumbled over with a bang that ricocheted down the alley, leaving an enormous drop between the window and the Dumpster. Nina's legs flailed frantically as her strong arms worked to pull her the rest of the way inside. The wooden window sash scraped along her belly. Ignoring the pain and the splinters stabbing her unprotected hands, Nina managed to wriggle through the window, falling at last onto the filthy brown carpet inside.

I'm dead, she thought, hurriedly rolling back onto her feet and crouching up against the wall beneath the window. *With all that noise someone must have seen me!* Holding her breath, Nina peered fearfully back out the window. But no one came running into the alley, no new lights sprang to life at the sudden commotion. *In this neighborhood they're probably used to it*, Nina realized, grateful just the same. After several more long, nervous minutes of watching, Nina figured she'd gotten away with breaking and entering. Or entering anyway.

"What a relief!" she breathed, rising slowly

to a standing position. Wouldn't it be ironic if she got sent to jail while that psycho Rachel still roamed the streets?

"Speaking of psychos," she muttered, remembering why she was there. Nina had come to look for clues. Clues about Rachel's intentions toward her, about her plans for Stu, about the baby she carried . . .

"Rachel Max, you're a cheap, lying criminal," Nina told the empty room. "And personally I don't believe a word you say. Maybe that's Stu's baby you're having, and maybe it's not. Stu's so trusting, he'll probably believe whatever you tell him."

Nina's dark eyes scanned the room suspiciously. "If it's all the same to you, Rachel, I think I'll have a look around."

Chapter Six

Gee, Ryan's the life of the party tonight, Jessica thought sarcastically, rolling her eyes as her dream date slopped down yet another beer.

I just don't get it, she continued silently. The evening had started out well enough. After Jessica met Ryan at the Main Tower, he'd driven them to the Cove for a romantic dinner. But after dinner Jessica had grown bored of sipping soft drinks and admiring the view. After all, there was only so much you could say about a sunset.

"Let's go dancing somewhere," she'd suggested, remembering the heat of Ryan's strong arms around her as they'd danced in his room the night before.

"Are you old enough to get into a club?" Ryan had asked, apparently forgetting she was the exact same age as Elizabeth—eighteen.

"We could go to Pure Juice."

Ryan shook his head. "No way am I dancing at a teenybopper club. The strongest thing they serve at Pure Juice is Coca-Cola Classic. No offense, Jess," he'd added quickly, reaching across the table and giving her hand an apologetic squeeze. "Anyway, I know a place we can go where they couldn't care less about ID."

And that was how they'd ended up at Louie's Liquor Lounge. In her worst nightmares Jessica could never have imagined herself in such a tacky place. The walls were stained a dirty, nicotine yellow, the floor was so filthy, she wasn't sure *what* color it used to be, and every chair in the bar was sticky orange plastic. At least she and Ryan had a table in the back, where no one could see them through the big front window.

"Mmm. There's nothing like a cold beer," Ryan announced, finishing off his pint. He motioned to the bartender for another almost before he set down the glass. "There's just nothing that tastes quite like it. Know what I mean?"

"You're so right," Jessica agreed cuttingly. "But soaking old gym socks in ginger ale comes pretty close."

Ryan simply laughed. "You're so funny, Jessica. *Nothing* like your sister. Elizabeth has no sense of humor at all."

I'm starting to see why, Jessica thought, clenching her jaw to keep from saying something really nasty. Where was the sexy, attentive Ryan of the night before? All *this* Ryan wanted to do was drink.

The bartender walked over and plunked down another beer, and Ryan slurped the foam off the top eagerly. *He's disgusting!* Jessica thought, turning her head away. How could she ever have been into this guy? But as her eyes roamed over the other people in the bar, Jessica couldn't help noticing how many of the women were looking at her and Ryan enviously, obviously wishing they were in her spiked white heels.

Maybe I should reconsider, Jessica told herself, turning her attention back to Ryan. He was still drinking beer, still oblivious to her boredom. Of course, what was there to do *but* drink in Louie's Liquor Lounge? There was no band, no view, no one interesting to talk to. Jessica shuddered with the knowledge that she was hanging out somewhere so woefully uncool.

"Hey, Ryan," she said suddenly. "Why don't we go someplace else? I'll drive," she added, holding out her hand for his car keys.

"What do you want to go somewhere else for?" Ryan asked, looking genuinely amazed. "This place is great!"

It's hopeless, Jessica realized, her shoulders sinking. All she wanted to do now was hurry home and let the nightmare end. "I've got to be at work bright and early tomorrow," she said, faking an enormous yawn, complete with arm stretching, for emphasis. "I think it's about time for me to get some sleep."

"Ahhh, it's not late!" Ryan protested.

Jessica pointed to the wall over the bar, where the most hideously ugly, twirling beer-logo clock she'd ever seen held the place of honor. "It's late enough," she said.

"*That's* not late!" Ryan scoffed. "Hey, I know what *you* want to do. *You* want to *dance*."

"I *wanted* to dance," Jessica corrected him. "About two hours ago."

"There's no time like the present!" Ryan declared loudly. He lurched out of his chair and grabbed Jessica by one arm, pulling her onto her feet. "Come on. Let's boogie!"

Boogie! Jessica could feel her face flaming with embarrassment as Ryan dragged her up to the front of the bar, where an ancient jukebox played what passed for music at Louie's. "Ryan, I don't want—"

"Oh yes, you do!" Ryan interrupted, spinning her around the floor. Mortified, Jessica closed her eyes to avoid having to make eye contact with anyone who might be watching. After only two quick turns, though, Ryan lost his balance, lurching drunkenly into the jukebox. The record skipped, and Ryan swore. To regain his equilibrium, he threw both arms around Jessica and leaned into her with all his considerable weight.

"Thass better," he slurred as Jessica staggered under the unexpected load.

"Better for who?" she asked sharply. "Stop it, Ryan! Stand up!"

He laid his slack cheek down on top of her head. "Don't you just love this song?"

"I don't know this song," Jessica answered angrily. "I don't think my *parents* know this song."

"The old love songs are the best," Ryan replied, unruffled, tightening his grip.

Jessica felt as if he were squeezing the air right out of her. "Ryan, I have to go," she said, reaching for the keys in his back pocket.

With surprising speed, considering the circumstances, Ryan intercepted her hand halfway to its destination and brought it up to his shoulder. "Not so fast, gorgeous. We still gotta whole night ahead of us."

Jessica stiffened, then relaxed against him. Obviously Ryan wasn't going anywhere voluntarily. Unless she wanted to make a scene in Louie's Liquor Lounge—and she *didn't*—she'd just have to wait him out. Jessica laid her face against his chest and closed her eyes again, wishing the night were over.

So much for my dream date, she mourned silently as Ryan whirled her sloppily around the tiny dance floor.

Rachel regarded her future husband through hard, suspicious eyes. "I thought you wanted to work this out," she told him, a dangerous edge in her voice.

"I do, but Rachel! We only spent one night together," Stuart protested. "I want to help, but I also want to be sure that . . . uh . . ." He paused and averted his eyes uncomfortably. "That it's mine," he finished softly. "I'm sorry, but before I can commit to anything more than money, I need to be sure of that."

Rachel relaxed, smiling and moving closer on Stuart's wide blue-and-green-striped couch. "Of *course* it's ours," she assured him, putting a hand on his leg and snuggling into his shoulder. "*He's* ours. We're going to have a boy."

It feels so good to be back on SeaMist Island, she told herself, smiling. *It feels like coming home. And this time Stuart finally* invited *me!* She stretched luxuriously on the sofa, hoping to give him the hint that it was time for bed.

"I guess we'll have to get a DNA test done," Stuart mused aloud.

"A *what?*" she screeched, bolting upright on the couch.

"Look, Rachel, if it's money you want, I've got plenty of that. I'll help you out either way. But if you're looking for a father for your child . . . well . . . then I'm going to need some proof that it's mine."

"You don't *believe* me?" Rachel cried, horrified. How could this be happening? The love she had with Stuart was bigger than tests, beyond petty assurances. He sounded so detached, so clinical, so very *un*-Stuart. Why was he acting this way?

Then suddenly Rachel knew. It was Nina!

Stuart pulled at the collar of his faded PacificaWear T-shirt. "I don't *not* believe you—"

"Stuart, I love you," Rachel blurted, taking his hands in hers. Her own hands were trembling, but she pressed ahead anyway. "And I forgive you. It's not your fault that Nina took advantage of you and forced herself between us. But I will *not* be treated this way, Stuart. This is our baby, and we're going to have it together."

Stuart's crystal blue eyes narrowed irritably. "Leave Nina out of it. She has nothing to do with this."

"Exactly!" Rachel purred contentedly, snuggling back into his shoulder. He finally got it! "Nina has nothing to do with this at all. And leaving her out of it is exactly what I have in mind."

Stuart was stiff and silent as Rachel held him on the sofa. She wished he'd loosen up a little— he was so shy! Not at all like that first night they'd met. Rachel closed her eyes, smiling at the memory of Stuart sweeping her into his arms, his eyes full of passion, needing her. Why wasn't he like that now?

Men are intimidated by pregnant women, she told herself, thinking she must have read that somewhere. *Stuart just needs time to get used to the idea that we're having a baby.*

At the thought of the baby Rachel's heart rose up in her chest. Their child would be so perfect. She could see it now—a towheaded carbon copy of Stuart. Blond, tan, and adorable, playing on its own private beach.

But what if the baby isn't *blond?* Rachel thought suddenly, disturbed. The baby had to look just like Stuart. What if it inherited her dark hair?

Ridiculous, she scoffed. *I'm blond too now. Of course his hair will be blond.* And if it wasn't, she'd bleach it. For that matter, maybe she'd keep bleaching hers too, so they'd all look alike—the perfect golden family.

In her mind's eye Rachel saw the three of them sitting on the beach next to Stuart's private dock. Everything would be set up perfectly—beach blankets, umbrellas, a picnic lunch. The baby would be toddling, playing with his toy pail and shovel.

David! she yelled lovingly in her imagination. *Don't go too close to the water. Mommy doesn't want you to fall in!*

And he would turn to her, little David, and smile like the sun. A wave of love swept over her; it was so beautiful and clear that Rachel shuddered with emotion.

"I want to name the baby David," she told Stuart, almost as an afterthought. "How does David sound to you?"

Stuart tensed under her fingers. "It seems a little early to be picking out names," he protested weakly, but Rachel paid no attention.

As far as she was concerned, it was already done. David Max Kirkwood. The perfect name for the perfect child.

She would have to get to work on decorating the baby's room right away, of course. Now, while she still had the energy, was the time to pick out new carpet, wallpaper, a crib. And toys—a roomful of toys. She and Stuart would give this baby everything.

"So when do you want me to move in?" she asked. "I could do it tomorrow. And I think the meditation room is the perfect room to fix up for the baby, don't you? I want to take everything out of there and—"

"Whoa!" Stuart interrupted. "First things first. There's the DNA test, for one thing. But even after that, I don't think you should move into this house until after your—*our* baby is born. The island is too isolated. What if . . . what if you were to need a doctor or something in the middle of the night?"

Rachel opened her mouth to lash into him, then changed her mind abruptly. After all, Stuart *had* just said "our baby" for the very first time. He was coming around.

"Whatever you think's best, Stuart," she cooed submissively, nuzzling his cheek. "But I'll have to stay here tonight. My car's completely out of gas."

"Out of gas?" Stuart repeated, pushing away

from her and looking into her eyes. "Why didn't you get gas before you came, Rachel? It's not like I have a gas station out here on the island."

"I didn't notice I was on empty until I was crossing the bridge, and at that point I didn't think I should turn around," Rachel lied. "I could have run out in the middle of nowhere!"

Stuart sighed as if exhausted, even though it was still early in the evening. "Well, we'll just have to see what we can find. I'm pretty sure I have a few spare gallons in the boathouse. If not, I can siphon some out of the tanks on the boat."

"But Stuart!" Rachel protested. "You're obviously too tired to do all that. Besides, wouldn't it be easier to siphon gas in the morning, when it's light?"

"No doubt. I wish you'd told me earlier." He rose wearily from the couch, shaking off Rachel's grasping hands. "Come on. Let's go check the boathouse."

"Stuart! No! Wouldn't you rather cuddle on the couch? Or we could go upstairs. . . ."

Stuart eyed her from the middle of the living room. More than anything Rachel longed to take him into her arms, to bury her hands in that thick sun-bleached hair.

"I'm going to the boathouse," he repeated obstinately. "You can wait here if you want, or you can help me gas up your car."

"I'll wait," Rachel said petulantly, throwing herself down full-length on the couch.

"Fine."

Stuart turned and walked out into the night. Rachel watched him through the windows as he headed down the softly lit path to the beach and boathouse.

Maybe I should have gone with him, she thought irresolutely. But she had so wanted to stay at the mansion! If she could only get Stuart to herself, get him alone for a single night, Rachel knew he'd never want her to leave his side again. It had been so easy last time. Why was he making it so hard now?

Rachel's eyes glinted dangerously as the answer came to her with sudden, blinding clarity. A muscle below her mouth twitched violently, contorting her face.

Nina Harper! she thought furiously. *When I get done with her, she's going to wish she'd never even laid eyes on my Stuart!*

Look at them dancing, Elizabeth thought, depression overwhelming her. *Jess looks so happy and beautiful. And Ryan's acting like the luckiest guy in the world. Obviously I'm not missed in the slightest.*

Elizabeth toyed with the key in the ignition of the red Jeep the twins shared, knowing she should leave but unable to make herself. From where she'd parked at the curb, she had an unobstructed view of the happy couple. They were framed in the wide front window of Louie's Liquor Lounge like a picture postcard of someone else's dream vacation.

He doesn't need you anymore, a voice in her head reminded her. *He's with Jessica now.* But the thought cut through Elizabeth like a freezing wind. Even if Ryan didn't love her anymore, she'd never be able to stop caring for him. And he was so vulnerable now, so on the edge. Could Jessica really be trusted to handle the situation? Take tonight, for example. Had Ryan been drinking? *At Louie's* Liquor *Lounge?* Elizabeth answered sarcastically. *Of* course *he's been drinking!*

Then, as she watched, Ryan stumbled slightly on the dance floor. Instinctively Elizabeth leaned forward, her arms aching to catch him. But it was Jessica who got the job, steadying Ryan gently, a compassionate smile on her face. Elizabeth slumped back into the driver's seat, her sore heart nearly breaking.

Why torture yourself this way? she asked herself miserably. *What do you hope to accomplish?* But it wasn't about accomplishing anything anymore, Elizabeth knew. She just couldn't bear to be parted from Ryan, to have their relationship be over forever. Besides, Jessica wouldn't watch out for Ryan the way she would have. Jessica wouldn't get him the help he needed.

Oh yeah. It was real helpful walking out on

him right when he needed you most, Elizabeth accused herself. How could she have done that? What genius had invented "tough love" anyway, and why had she been stupid enough to try it?

But you had to do something to make your point, Elizabeth argued internally. *You had to show Ryan you didn't approve of what he was doing.*

"He *knew* I didn't approve of his drinking," she answered back as the tears rolled down her cheeks. "I should have shown him how much I loved him instead!"

Again Elizabeth played with the key in the ignition, trying to work up the resolve to leave. It was a fluke that she'd stumbled onto Jessica and Ryan in the first place—she desperately wished she hadn't. Elizabeth had been driving to the grocery store when she'd noticed Ryan's distinctive, racing-orange Datsun 240Z parked on a seedy side street. She'd been so shocked to see the classic car in such a scummy area that she'd turned the corner on reflex, only to encounter the sight in front of her now.

Ryan and Jessica.

The happy new couple.

Yanking savagely at her door handle, she stormed out of the Jeep, a renewed sense of anger coursing through her. She'd tell them both what she thought of them. She didn't care *how* big a scene she made!

But when Elizabeth was halfway to the door,

she stopped dead in her tracks. Ryan had pulled Jessica tightly against him and was kissing her deeply, in full sight of everyone in the bar. His lips worked passionately against her sister's as his hands wandered over Jessica's scantily dressed frame.

Elizabeth stood frozen on the sidewalk, horrified. She couldn't go in there now! Everyone would see how jealous she was!

As the kiss between Ryan and Jessica continued, becoming embarrassing in its length and intensity, Elizabeth fidgeted, knowing they couldn't see her through the glare off the windows. She felt like a voyeur.

Maybe I should just go in and tell Jessica to come home, she thought, desperate for a plausible excuse to break things up. *Jess has to work tomorrow, and it's getting late. She needs her sleep.*

But Jessica was *still* clasped tightly in Ryan's arms. The embrace continued until Jessica's hands dropped casually below Ryan's waist, settling comfortably over his two back pockets. Elizabeth's mouth dropped open in shock, but Ryan simply smiled approvingly and kissed his new girlfriend all over again.

Elizabeth wheeled around on the sidewalk and hurried back to the Jeep, unable to watch any longer. She couldn't believe that Ryan Taylor was acting so totally, publicly love struck. And with Jessica instead of with her! Fresh tears stung Elizabeth's eyes, and she fought to swallow past a hard lump in her throat as she climbed shakily into the driver's seat.

He's drunk, she reminded herself. *He probably doesn't even know what he's doing*.

"Yeah? So what's Jessica's excuse?" she countered bitterly, turning the key in the Jeep's ignition. The engine roared and Elizabeth peeled away from the curb in a fury, not caring that she'd just left half the rubber off her tires behind her on the pavement. The last thing Elizabeth saw was Ryan's orange 240Z in her rearview mirror.

I hope he lets Jessica drive.

The thought came to her suddenly, unwelcomely. Ryan shouldn't be driving in his condition. But knowing Ryan as she did, he wasn't too likely to turn his car keys over either. As much as she didn't want to think about it, Elizabeth couldn't help worrying how they'd get home.

Angrily Elizabeth swiped at the tears that streamed down both sides of her face. *That's Jessica's problem*, she decided fiercely. *She made this bed. It's time for her to wake up in it!*

This is hardly Better Homes and Gardens *material*, Nina thought, wrinkling her nose in distaste as she looked around Rachel's tiny, squalid apartment. *Maybe* Weirder Kooks and Stalkers *would be interested in doing a spread*. Nina had half expected to find a voodoo doll in her likeness stuck full of pins or something, but so far all she'd seen was a dirty one-room apartment so pathetic and depressing that Nina could almost cry.

Almost.

This girl's out to get you, she reminded herself. *Save your sympathy for someone who deserves it!*

Still, it was weird to think that Rachel had fallen so far in the world. Only the summer before she'd been the captain of the South Beach Squad. *And a top-notch lifeguard,* Nina couldn't help remembering, *even if she was only a subaverage human being.*

"Well, this isn't getting me anywhere," Nina whispered, shaking off the spell that had come over her. "I ought to be looking for clues."

Not that Nina expected her search to take very long. Rachel's apartment contained a rickety-looking single bed, a desk, a few unpacked cardboard boxes, and little else. Nina could call out for a pizza, eat the whole thing herself, and still have time to memorize every item in the room before Rachel got back from Stu's house.

Heaving a sigh, Nina studied the unmade bed. "Maybe there's something under the mattress," she muttered. Holding the thin, lumpy mattress by only the tips of her fingers, Nina lifted it and looked underneath. Nothing.

"What exactly are you expecting to find anyway?" she asked herself as she dropped the mattress back into position. She didn't even know. A gun, maybe, or some type of weapon. Something that would let her know if Rachel intended to keep stalking her—and how far she planned to go.

Finding a diary would be like hitting the mother lode. With a diary Nina could find out everything. Whether or not Stu was really the father of Rachel's baby, for example, and what Rachel planned to do about it. Did she want to marry Stu? Or was this some kind of twisted scheme to extort money? Anything seemed possible.

Nina lifted a rumpled bath towel off the top of one of the boxes and began poking through its contents: shabby, yard-sale clothes and mismatched linens. Nina moved on through a second box, then a third, finding nothing of any interest. The fourth box, a small one, held Rachel's makeup and bathroom things.

"This stuff could belong to anyone!" Nina exclaimed, so frustrated she forgot to keep quiet. There was nothing personal in the boxes at all. No letters, no photos, no books. Nothing. She dismissed the boxes and turned toward the desk. "You're my last chance," she told it, yanking open the top drawer.

"Oh, good. Underwear," she muttered sarcastically when she saw what it contained. "Nice place to put it."

Nina rifled through the contents of the drawer anyway, just to be sure, but found only socks and underwear. The second drawer held two folded housecoats. The third drawer was empty. "Come *on!*" She groaned, tugging at the fourth and final drawer.

The drawer flew open, and Nina's eyes widened. The space was nearly empty, but carefully placed at the back were two photographs—one faceup in each corner. The area between them was littered with scraps of pink paper, as if several larger sheets had been torn into tiny pieces and dumped there.

"What have we here?" She reached for the first photo and lifted it up to the light. A much younger and glowingly happy Rachel stood with her arm slung around the shoulders of a boy roughly her own age. They both looked to be about nine or ten, but that wasn't what caught her attention about the picture.

It was the boy.

Wearing only cutoff blue jeans, the boy mugged goofily for the camera, his crystal blue eyes shining with laughter. The kid's shaggy, sun-bleached hair stood out in all directions, and the whiteness of his smile was shocking against his dark, golden tan.

He looks like Stu, Nina thought, feeling a chill run from between her shoulder blades all the way down to her calves. *Eerily like Stu.*

Nina's hand trembled as she replaced the first photograph and reached for the second. It was a school picture of the boy, his wild blond hair combed for the camera. Cleaned up and close-up, his resemblance to Stu was even more uncanny.

What year was this taken? Nina wondered, flipping the photograph over. But instead of a date a loopy, childish scrawl met Nina's eyes: *To Ray-Ray. Best Friends Forever! David.*

Nina's breath came out in a relieved rush. For a second there she'd almost believed the boy in the photos *was* Stu. In spite of the large age difference they looked so much alike, it was frightening.

"David," she breathed, tracing the name on the back of the photograph with one finger. Nina hesitated a moment, then stuffed the picture into her back shorts pocket.

I wonder what these are? she thought, scooping up a handful of the pink paper scraps from the drawer and gazing at them curiously, unsure if it was worth her trouble to piece them together.

"Well, I've come this far," she muttered under her breath, depositing the handful of scraps on the barren desktop and looking for pieces that matched. It took Nina only a few minutes to realize she was looking at the torn results of some type of hospital laboratory test.

And I'll bet I know exactly what type of test old Rachel went in for! she thought, her heart pounding with excitement. The minutes flew by as Nina painstakingly reassembled every last piece of the puzzle. When she was done, she stood back from the desk and stared disbelievingly at the evidence in front of her: four pregnancy tests, several weeks apart.

All negative.

"It's a trick!" Nina gasped. "She's not even *having* a baby."

In a single, shaking motion Nina scooped up the scraps and dropped them back into the drawer. Stu was supposed to telephone her at the beach house the minute Rachel left. And after what she'd just found out, Nina wanted to make sure she was home to take that call. She had to warn him.

Turning back the dead bolt on Rachel's front door, Nina hurried out into the night.

Chapter
Seven

"You're so sweet. D'jya know that?" Ryan slurred as Jessica dug through his pockets in search of the car keys. "Wha' would I do wi'out you?"

"Probably walk," Jessica returned irately. Finding the keys at last, she yanked them from Ryan's pocket and quickly opened the passenger door. "There. Now get in."

She'd expected him to argue, but Ryan was so wasted that he flowed down into the seat as if there were no bones left in his body. "Sure thing, Jessie," he said, leering at her drunkenly. "Hey! Whaddya say we go back t'my place?"

Jessica leaned down into the tiny sports car, struggling to fasten Ryan's seat belt across his lap. "Go stuff yourself," she muttered as the buckle finally clicked into place.

"Whassat?"

Jessica ignored him. "I'm taking you home,

but I'm not staying with you." She straightened up and slammed the passenger-side door shut.

"You'll change your mind when we get there," Ryan predicted, sticking his head through the open window.

Fat chance, Jessica thought. She hurried around the car to the driver's side, but when she reached the driver's door, she paused irresolutely. Ryan's 240Z was in flawless condition, and Jessica was suddenly worried about driving it. What if she accidentally ground the gears? Or hit a pothole?

She chewed her lip anxiously, imagining the possibilities. Would Ryan be mad at her if something happened to his car? "Who cares," she told herself, flinging open the driver's door and dropping into the seat. After all, there was no way she could handle the car any worse than Ryan at the moment.

"Are we going back to the Main Tower?" Ryan asked as Jessica started the engine.

"I just said we were," she snapped. Jessica studied the gearshift and on-dash controls, making sure she knew where everything was. She found the headlights and switched them on. She was reaching to put the car into gear when Ryan intercepted her hand, pulling it up to his sloppy lips.

"I'm gonna show you a night you'll never ferget," he promised, waggling his eyebrows at her in a maneuver he seemed to think was sexy. Then he belched. Jerking her hand free of his,

Jessica shifted the car into gear and pulled out into the street. "You already have," she told him, disgusted beyond belief. A second later the radio switched on unexpectedly, practically blasting Jessica out of her seat.

"Wha' we need's some *tunes!*" Ryan declared, fiddling with the presets. "Sumpin' romantic."

"Turn that down!" Jessica screamed over the music. "I'm trying to drive!"

Ryan looked confused. "Tryin' to dive?" he repeated, his forehead wrinkled with concentration. "Doan you wanna wait'll we get back to the beach?"

"Stop it!" Jessica slapped his hand away from the radio and turned down the volume herself. "Now leave that alone."

But Ryan seemed to have lost interest in the radio. Instead he rolled his window the rest of the way down and stuck his head halfway out into the wind like the dog he had become.

"Too bad I didn't bring a muzzle," Jessica muttered to herself, glancing at Ryan with distaste. She could still barely believe what a nightmare her so-called dream date had turned into. Not only had she been totally humiliated to be seen in that dive bar, but also, to make things worse, she was going to have to face Miranda in the morning and admit how horrible her evening had been.

Unless she lied, of course.

Jessica looked over to where Ryan's head still lolled drunkenly out the window.

She'd obviously have to lie.

I just don't understand how he got so drunk, she thought. *Ryan had a few shots of whiskey last night and he was fine. How could only twice as many beers do him in this way?* Jessica made the turn onto the main road along the coast. *Maybe . . . maybe if he's been drinking all day . . .*

The full consequences of that appalling scenario dawned on Jessica gradually. Could Elizabeth have been telling the *truth?* Was it possible that Ryan really *did* have a drinking problem? Jessica stared at her date in horror, expecting drool to start dribbling from his slack mouth any second. The way he'd been carrying on all night, a drinking problem didn't seem impossible.

No! Jessica reprimanded herself immediately, forcing the thought from her mind. *No! Don't you see? You're playing right into Elizabeth's hands. That's what she* wants *you to think. She's trying to poison you against him.*

Ten minutes later the Main Tower came into view. Jessica nudged the sports car over the speed bump at the entrance to the parking lot, but the 240Z bounced sharply in spite of her caution. The sudden movement seemed to jolt Ryan out of his stupor. He turned to her, blinking as if just waking up. When his eyes finally focused, though, they were surprisingly clear. Not only that, but the gaze he leveled at her was incredibly intense, brimming with barely suppressed emotion.

"I love you," he said urgently, grabbing for her hand as the car rolled to a stop. "I know this isn't the time or the place, but I hafta say it now. B'fore I lose my nerve."

Jessica's eyebrows shot up in surprise. What had come over *him* all of a sudden? Ryan was acting like his old, unbelievably charming self again—only better. Much, much better.

Now this *is more like it,* she thought, flattered into letting him hold her hand. Apparently he'd sobered up on the long drive home. Jessica smiled at him encouragingly, smitten in spite of their earlier disastrous date.

"I know this isn't wha' we planned, and I know I shouldn'ta been drinkin' tonight, but I do love you." Ryan leaned forward and kissed her gently, his lips just barely brushing hers. "Whaddever else happens, I want you to know that, Elizabeth."

Jessica's heart dropped through the floorboards. *"Elizabeth!"* she screeched, snatching her hand out of his. "Get out! Get out of the car this instant!"

"Whaddaye say?" Ryan slurred as Jessica reached across him and opened his door. She half pushed, half kicked him out of the car, her high heel sinking into his side.

"E*liz*abeth . . . ," he whined from the pavement.

"*Elizabeth* is going home," Jessica spat, slamming the passenger door. "You can walk over and pick up your car tomorrow." Grinding the gears, Jessica tore out of the parking lot, smirking with satisfaction when Ryan's precious 240Z bottomed out on the speed bump. As furious as she was, she seriously considered backing up and taking the bump again.

I can't believe *he called me Elizabeth*, she thought irately as she drove home to the beach house. *Of all the insults!*

But what Jessica *really* wanted to know was whether Ryan had actually thought she was Elizabeth or whether he was just so wasted that he'd mixed up the names without realizing it. Either thing seemed possible. *He's so drunk, he could have mistaken me for Princess Di*, Jessica told herself.

Still, it hurt to think that Ryan might only be hanging out with her because she reminded him of her sister. Jessica's knuckles turned white on the wheel, and she had to take several deep breaths to keep from crying. Ryan *couldn't* still have a thing for Elizabeth. Could he?

Just forget about it, Jessica advised herself savagely, punching the accelerator for emphasis. *It was one wasted night. The next time you'll keep him in line.*

And there was going to be a next time. There *had* to be. There was no way Jessica Wakefield was going to admit to the world that she'd already struck out *twice* in the romance department—and with the summer barely under way!

"OK. I think you're starting to get it, but we'd better practice a few more times just to be sure." Winston scooped up the crystals quickly before Pedro could say no.

"Winston, I'm *tired!*" Pedro moaned. "I just flew in from *Sweden*. Do you understand about foreign time zones at all? I can't do this anymore. Not tonight."

Winston ignored Pedro's protests, hurriedly rearranging the crystals on the low glass table between them. From his position in the Queen Anne chair, Winston was pretending to be Wendy in order to put Pedro, the newly christened Guru Futi, through all his cosmic paces. "One more time," Winston urged. "Here. What does this pattern suggest?"

Pedro glanced at the crystals and then up at Winston, his brown eyes weary and bloodshot. "It suggests I'm going to wring your neck if you don't let me get some sleep," he answered darkly. "I'm not kidding, Winston."

Winston gulped. Pedro sure didn't *look* like he was kidding. "Well, all right," he agreed reluctantly. "But I really think that—"

"Save it for tomorrow."

Pedro got up, stretched, and walked stiffly

into the bedroom. "Good night," he called once he was out of sight. A second later the light in the bedroom flicked off, leaving Winston alone in the living room.

It'll be OK, Winston reassured himself, putting away the crystals. *Pedro will be more on top of things tomorrow when he's not so tired.*

But secretly Winston was scared. Pedro wasn't turning out to be a very convincing guru. Sure, the clothes were great, and the hotel suite looked just right. But all of those props were wasted if Pedro couldn't pull off the acting job.

Restlessly Winston rose from the chair, walked to the French doors, and opened them onto the terrace. It was late—past midnight—and the breeze off the ocean was sharp and cold. Winston stepped out onto the patio anyway and sat in one of the deeply cushioned lounge chairs, covering himself with a couple of enormous hotel beach towels. It felt good, sitting out under the stars, the fresh air clearing his head. Winston closed his eyes, thinking about his plans for the following day.

He'd promised Wendy that he'd play tennis in the morning and take her out to lunch. Then, at sunset, he and Wendy had an appointment with "Guru Futi." Hopefully Pedro would do some practicing in the meantime because Winston wasn't going to be able to help him anymore. Once Wendy got Winston in her sights, she'd definitely keep him busy all day.

"Wendy." Winston sighed, snuggling down farther into the lounge chair. Was she really in love with him like she said? Winston remembered how intense, how certain Wendy's eyes had been when she'd uttered those words.

She was out of her mind, he told himself, not liking how the memory made him hot all over. *After all, she's married, and I'm with Denise. She didn't know what she was saying.*

But what if she did?

For the very first time Winston allowed himself to imagine being with Wendy Paloma. Even the thought made his heart beat faster. He liked her—he'd always liked her. Maybe Wendy wasn't the prettiest girl he knew, but she more than made up for that with her sense of humor and, now that she had money, her unexpected sense of style. Winston wasn't a fool; he knew he was no prize in the looks department himself. But the fact that Wendy—a superstar's wife—would even *consider* dating him really warped his mind.

But do you love *her?* he asked himself before he could stop the question.

No. I don't know. Maybe. Winston tugged at his makeshift blankets in annoyance, gathering them high up under his chin. *What about Denise?*

Denise. How could he ever betray his sweet Denise? Not to mention Pedro. It wouldn't even be fair to Wendy—not in the confused state she was in.

No. Wendy Paloma is definitely out, Winston decided. The thought made him a little sad, but the more overwhelming emotion by far was relief. Now that he'd taken the time to think it over, in fact, the entire notion seemed insane. Winston wished Wendy had never put it into his head.

So then forget it. Tomorrow Wendy and Pedro will get back together, and everyone will live happily ever after.

Winston flipped over onto his side, surprised at how comfortable it was on the patio. Somewhere out there, far away in the darkness, waves crashed onto the beach, but only a hushed, muted roar reached Winston's ears. It would be so peaceful to doze off there, surrounded by a million stars. Unfortunately Wendy had no idea where he was. She was probably worried sick, and Winston knew he'd have to leave for the Paloma house in a minute.

Nah. Wendy's probably sound asleep by now. There's no hurry. Winston breathed in the cool night air drowsily, barely aware that he was drifting off to sleep.

Ring already, Nina mentally commanded her silent alarm clock. It *had* to be time to get up by now. Already the Friday morning sunshine filtered through her blinds, promising another busy day at the beach. More important, Nina was supposed to see Stu before her lifeguard shift began.

"That's it. I can't wait anymore." She threw off the covers impatiently. But once she was up on her feet, Nina saw the reason the alarm hadn't sounded yet—it was barely six o'clock.

I don't care, she told herself, stepping into her red bathing suit anyway. *There's no way I can sleep when I'm this wound up.* She found the navy blue sweatpants that were part of the squad's cold-day uniform and pulled them on over her suit, finishing up with the regulation Windbreaker and a pair of sneakers. Then she took Rachel's photograph of David off her nightstand and zipped it into a jacket pocket. "Good enough," she said, hurrying out of her bedroom and into the bathroom.

Ever since she'd left Rachel's apartment the night before, Nina had been a nervous wreck. Stu hadn't called until after midnight, and when he had, the stories he'd told were as scary as Nina's own: Rachel wanted to move in with him, Rachel had made a transparent play to spend the night, Rachel had already named their nonexistent baby.

Nina shuddered as she hurriedly ran a brush through her straightened black hair. If she and Stu didn't come up with some type of plan, there was no telling what that psycho would do. Up until now Rachel had held all the cards, called all the shots. It was time to turn that trend around.

Downstairs, Nina slipped silently out the back door. A few minutes later she was on her bike, pedaling hard toward SeaMist Island. Stu had promised to meet her at the Main Tower an hour before her shift started, but Nina didn't want to wait that long. She wanted to see Stu *now*, put her arms around him *now*.

The miles rolled by under Nina's bicycle as her strong legs pumped automatically, almost without effort. Before she knew it, she was crossing the bridge, then rolling up the driveway to Stu's adobe beach house.

"Nina!" Stu called worriedly, walking out the front door while she was dismounting from the bike. "What are you doing here? Is something the matter?" He still looked half asleep, and his plaid flannel pajama pants rode low on his muscular hips. Nina could see the sheet marks still crisscrossing his broad, tan chest, and his hair stood out as wildly as the boy's hair in the photo.

"Oh, Stu!" she cried, dropping the bike and running into his warm, reassuring arms. "Stu, I was so worried!"

"About me?" he asked, his blue eyes clouding. "Or did she do something else to you? I swear, if—"

"No. I'm fine. It's just that I'm so weirded out by this whole thing. I . . . I really needed to see you."

"Me too. Come on, let's talk about this in the house."

Stu led Nina into the kitchen, where a breakfast of assorted fruit lay half prepared on the cutting board. "Here, have some pineapple," he urged, pushing the choicest chunks into a ceramic bowl and setting it at the breakfast bar. "It's great for digestive cleansing."

"Thanks," Nina said weakly, dropping onto the stool in front of the bowl. Cleansing or not, she was sure she'd never be able to eat Stu's pineapple with her stomach in knots. "Look. Here's the picture I told you about last night." She drew the photo carefully out of her jacket pocket and handed it over. "Look at the back too."

Stu glanced at the photograph, and his mouth fell open in amazement. He gazed at the boy's image a long, long time before he turned the picture over and read the back.

"See?" said Nina, pointing to the inscription. "David. The same thing Rachel wants to name your so-called baby."

"This is seriously freaked." Stu flipped the picture back over. "This kid looks *exactly* like I did when I was his age."

"But it's not you," Nina said. She had intended it to be a statement, but it came out sounding more like a question.

"No. Of course not," Stu said. "But I have to admit, if my *mother* handed me this picture

114

and said it was me, I'd believe her without thinking twice. It's creepy."

"What is Rachel trying to pull?" Nina asked, frustrated by her own confusion. "None of it makes any sense! She's not pregnant, but she says she is. Apparently she wants to have a baby and name it after some guy who looks just like you. If it was anyone else, I'd say she's after your money. But with Rachel . . . who knows?"

"I don't get the feeling this is about money," Stu said with a slight shudder. "You didn't see the way she was acting last night."

Nina grimaced, not even wanting to think about Rachel and Stu alone together, let alone Rachel crawling all over him, sinking her claws into him.

"Hey," Nina said suddenly. "Do you think this really *could* be a picture of you, and that Rachel got hold of it somehow and wrote that David stuff on the back?"

"Where would she have found such an old photograph of me?" Stu asked, shaking his head. "Especially one that I've never seen before. And anyway, you said there was another photo of Rachel with this same kid."

"Oh yeah."

"This isn't me," Stu concluded, dropping the photo onto the counter. "But one thing's for sure—you'd better stay here tonight. This whole situation is full of negative vibes, and . . . and I don't trust Rachel. I don't want you to be alone, just in case she—"

"Don't." Nina shuddered. "Don't say it."

It wasn't as if the thought hadn't occurred to Nina too. Rachel was just crazy enough to be dangerous, and she'd already snuck into Nina's room at the beach house. The thought of Rachel creeping up on her when she was sound asleep and helpless made Nina's blood run cold.

"But you will stay?" Stu insisted, wrapping his arms around her. "I want you to be safe."

"I'll stay," Nina answered gratefully, tracing the tattoo on his biceps. "I might even make you breakfast in the morning."

Rachel cursed from her position in the tall weeds across from Stuart's beach house. That predator Nina had just whisked Stuart off into the kitchen, where Rachel wasn't able to hear what they said. She could see them, though, through the big bay windows, sitting at the breakfast bar and looking nice and cozy. *Well, I've had enough of this lurking around outside,* Rachel decided angrily. *And I've had more than enough of Nina Harper!*

Rachel crept toward the house, keeping low and out of sight. Why was *she* out in the cold while Nina made herself comfortable in the kitchen? If things had gone according to plan, Rachel would have been moving in this morning, but instead it was *Nina* moving in—moving in on Rachel's future husband.

I hate her, Rachel told herself, creeping closer and closer. *I hate her, I hate her, I hate her!* Soon she was at the edge of the brush, and her only choices were to stay where she was or make a run for the garage.

Rachel ran, her heart pounding, expecting to hear someone shout any second. But nobody lifted a finger to stop her. *I should have known Stuart and Nina were too into each other to notice a little detail like someone sprinting up the driveway,* Rachel thought, covering the distance easily. She pressed up against the big garage door, making herself as flat as possible while considering her next move.

The next move would be to go in, of course. Maybe a back door's unlocked. Rachel slipped stealthily around the side of the garage until she reached the outside door to the laundry room. Very slowly, very carefully, she tried the knob. It turned easily in her sweaty hand, and the door swung open on silent hinges.

Perfect! It figures Stuart wouldn't lock his doors, Rachel thought as she crept through the laundry room. *I'll have to train him out of that Zen nonsense once we're married. Stuart can't be leaving doors unlocked with a baby in the house.*

Rachel froze where she stood and put both hands over her stomach, scared stiff by the thought of an intruder threatening her beautiful baby. How could Stuart be so thoughtless of David's safety? Her breathing came in fast, shallow gasps and the room dissolved around her as Rachel imagined David in danger, David hurt, David—

No! she warned herself harshly, struggling desperately to regain control. *Don't go there. Don't even think about it. Concentrate on why you're here. Concentrate on Nina.*

Nina. Rachel's eyes narrowed with hatred, and her breathing gradually slowed. Nina had been in her apartment last night. Rachel was sure of it. When she'd gotten back from Stuart's house, the dead bolt on her front door had been unlocked—a complete giveaway. It had taken only a second of searching to discover that her best picture of David was missing, stolen by that soulless home wrecker. Did she even know what a treasure she had?

I'll get it back, Rachel promised herself, sneaking toward the inside laundry-room door. *And I'll get Nina back too.*

The laundry room opened into a hall. Rachel struggled to remember the layout of this part of the house, but she'd seen it only once before, and that had been long ago. Too long ago.

Holding her breath, Rachel edged carefully down the hall, passing bedrooms and bathrooms as she worked her way toward the kitchen. At last she heard voices—Nina and Stuart. Rachel tiptoed closer, as close as she dared, ducking inside the doorway of the bathroom closest to the kitchen. The blood in her ears pounded so loudly that at first Rachel couldn't make out what was being said. Then Nina's voice came through to her, as sharp as a razor in enemy hands.

"See?" Nina was saying to Stuart. "David. The same thing Rachel wants to name your so-called baby."

So-called baby? Rachel wanted to leap screaming from her hiding place to tell the world that Nina was a liar. And what was she implying anyway? That Rachel wasn't pregnant? Of course she was. She *was!* Those hospitals didn't know anything. Their lab technicians were total idiots. How could they say she wasn't pregnant when Rachel could feel Stuart's baby growing inside her? She could *feel* it! They were wrong. Every single one of them.

With an effort Rachel restrained herself from running into the kitchen and confronting them both. Now wasn't the time—she wasn't prepared. *Besides, it will be better if Stuart never finds out exactly what happened to his precious Nina,* Rachel thought, soothing herself by imagining several possible bloody fates. Because Nina had to die now, of course. Rachel really couldn't see any alternative. Not that she'd *mind* tying up that little loose end, that final obstacle to her eternal happiness. She'd do what she had to do gladly. She'd do it with enthusiasm. There were no limits to what she was willing to do for Stuart.

The knowledge calmed her. As Rachel's erratic breathing slowed she gradually became aware of the voices again.

"But you will stay?" Stuart was asking, his voice full of misplaced concern. "I want you to be safe."

"I'll stay," Nina simpered in that nauseating, love-struck voice of hers. "I might even make you breakfast in the morning."

That scheming witch! Rachel raged, angry tears streaming down her face and falling unheeded to the floor beneath her feet. *OK, you go ahead and stay, Nina. But you won't be safe. You'll never be safe again!*

Chapter Eight

"Winston, where have you *been?*" Wendy demanded as Winston skidded wildly into the kitchen at the Paloma beach house. "You were gone all *day* yesterday. What time did you finally come in last night?"

"Oh, um, late," Winston replied evasively. *Like about five minutes ago,* he added silently.

Winston had woken up on Pedro's hotel lounge chair, cramped and cold, to the sound of seagulls fighting over something that had washed up on the beach. When he'd opened his eyes, he'd been horrified to see that the sun was already climbing the sky and that he'd slept through the entire night.

"Wendy's going to kill me!" he'd gasped, imagining her pacing the floor, calling all over town trying to find him. Without waking Pedro, Winston had thrown off his beach towel blankets and sprinted out of the hotel, running all the way back to the guest house at Wendy's. He was stripped before the water from the showerhead hit the shower floor, washed almost before he was wet, and dressed in clean shorts and a bowling shirt two seconds later. Then he'd raced to the kitchen, hoping to give the impression that everything was normal.

He wasn't sure, but it was starting to look like he'd gotten away with it.

"But where were you?" Wendy repeated, her hands on her nightgown-clad hips. "I *missed* you."

Wendy's gown was long and sleeveless, sewn of a thin white silk that shimmered teasingly over curves Winston hadn't known she had. He felt cold sweat trickling down his neck, then realized it was actually runoff from his soaking wet hair. Regardless, he bustled into the spacious, gourmet kitchen and grabbed a copper frying pan from its hook over the center island.

"I was just . . . uh . . . looking for another job. Eggs?" he asked brightly, holding up the pan.

Wendy stepped forward, took the pan from his hand, and set it carefully on the counter. "You *always* make me breakfast, Winston," she said, smiling. "This morning I've got it covered. Look."

Wendy pointed in the direction of the breakfast nook, and Winston turned his head obediently. The sheer white curtains there had been opened to their limits, exposing a spectacular view of crashing surf below the house. The sunlight that flooded through the windows made the expensive silver on the table glow, even while it sparkled off the cut crystal glasses and serving pieces. The dining table was draped in a heavy white damask cloth, and intricately folded pink linen napkins decorated two place settings of Wendy's wedding china.

"Isn't it romantic?" Wendy asked, slipping her bare arms around Winston from behind. "I did it all myself."

"Uh, nice," Winston managed, trying to wriggle free without being obvious. There were *flowers* on the table, he saw now, and champagne. Meanwhile Wendy was pressing her body against his, nothing between them but a damp bowling shirt and a microscopic layer of white silk.

"It's so nice to have a man in the house again," she murmured, laying her cheek on his back.

Blood rushed to Winston's face. "Wow, I'm starved!" he announced loudly, moving toward the breakfast table. "Let's chow down!"

Wendy relinquished her hold, and Winston hurried to sit at the table before she could change her mind and grab him again.

"'Chowing down' isn't very romantic, Winston," she complained as she slipped gracefully into the seat across from his.

Not very romantic? Winston answered silently. *Good.* He grabbed nervously for a pastry, then started loading fruit onto his plate. "Killer grub," he commented.

Wendy winced. "There's cream to go with those strawberries," she said, nudging the appropriate dish in Winston's direction. Her gray eyes looked less amorous, and Winston almost sighed with relief.

Situation almost normal, he thought. *Just a few final touches . . .*

He slathered cream cheese over a bagel, sculpted a sky-high mound of scrambled eggs next to that, then delivered the antiromance coup de grâce. "Where's the ketchup?" he asked, looking around the table. "No, don't move. I'll get it." Winston leaped from his seat, and a few moments later an industrial-size plastic bottle of ketchup towered among the silver and crystal, competing with the flowers for the honor of being centerpiece.

"So, um, did you get the job?" Wendy asked, the light in her eyes quenched completely. "I mean, the one you were applying for yesterday?"

Winston smiled with glee as he shoveled in a massive forkful of eggs. "No," he replied, chewing. "It wasn't the right position for me."

Wendy averted her eyes, clearly disgusted by his table manners.

No point in repulsing the poor girl further, he thought, putting down his fork and swallowing. "I just don't understand why people aren't lining up to give me jobs," he told her, meaning it.

"After all, I'm a smart guy. But every summer I end up dressed like a human hamburger or selling ice cream to juvenile delinquents. I don't get it."

Wendy smiled sympathetically. "You *are* a smart guy," she agreed. "Way too good to waste your time working at a job that's beneath you. It's a blessing you got fired from that Frost-ee-Freez gig."

"Yeah? Well, I felt more stressed than blessed when the cops were hauling me off to jail," Winston cracked. "Who knew that driving an ice-cream truck without a commercial license was such a big deal? I'm glad you were there to bail me out and get those charges cleared up and everything. Knowing the local celebrities has its advantages, I guess."

"If you can't pull a couple of strings for a friend once in a while, then what good are you?" Wendy teased, but her eyes looked more than "friendly" again. "I'd do anything for you, Winston," she added seriously. "You know that."

"Good. Remember you said so, because I got us an appointment with that new guru I told you about. He'll see us at seven o'clock tonight."

"Winston!" Wendy protested. "No more crackpots! I already told you that."

"Nope," Winston corrected, a sly smile on his face. "You just said you'd do *anything* for me."

"Anything but that," Wendy amended.

"Too late," Winston said cheerfully. "I heard you the first time."

"But Winston—"

"But nothing. Do you know how lucky I was to even get us an appointment? This guy is so hot that major movie stars are flying in to see him. They say he's never wrong."

"Wrong about what?" Wendy asked skeptically. "The total amount of your bill?"

"Very funny," Winston said, realizing how similar Wendy and Pedro's attitudes were on the whole psychic issue. "This guy happens to be tops in his field. He's a channeler."

"A channeler?" Wendy repeated, her eyebrows raised.

"He divines your true feelings and mentally channels them to the person you need to communicate with," Winston explained, hoping he sounded convincing. "Then he channels back their true response. He can put you in touch with Pedro."

"So could AT&T, if Pedro knew how to use a telephone."

"But this is *better* than a telephone," Winston insisted. "Guru Futi can tell you how Pedro feels in his *heart,* not just what he'd say over a long-distance line."

"Well, I hope he can channel surf all the way to Sweden, then, because that's where Pedro was the last time I spoke to his publicist."

"That's not going to matter! Guru Futi can do it."

"Winston, why are you doing this? You know I don't care anymore." Wendy dropped her gaze. "It's over with me and Pedro."

"Just talk to this one last guy," Winston begged, reaching impulsively for his friend's hand across the table. "If seeing Guru Futi doesn't change your mind, nothing will."

Truer words were never spoken, Winston added silently, wincing at the realization.

Wendy nodded reluctantly, and the tears she obviously hadn't wanted to shed began to overflow. "It's just so hard to keep discussing such totally personal feelings. You know?"

"I know. But it's going to be OK, Wendy," Winston soothed, his own heart aching as he stroked her hand. "I promise I'll make it OK if it takes me the rest of my life."

Wendy looked up, smiling slightly in spite of her tears. "How, exactly, do you think you can save someone else's failed marriage?"

Winston shrugged innocently. "You'd be surprised."

"I didn't think things could possibly get any better between me and Ryan, but last night was *unbelievable*," Jessica lied, trying her hardest to sound like the happiest girl in the world. It was just after lunchtime on Friday afternoon, and she and Miranda were lifeguarding from the Siberia of Tower 4

127

again, the sun dazzling on the hot sand around them.

"So what did you guys do?" Miranda asked. "Was it totally romantic?"

"Oh yeah!" Jessica fibbed again. After all, the first part of the evening had been OK, so it wasn't as if she was lying with abandon. "We went to the Cove for dinner, and then we . . . uh, went dancing."

"Dancing?" Miranda repeated, her wide brown eyes soaking up every detail. "Where?"

"At this really quiet, really intimate little club Ryan knows about. I . . . uh, forget what it's called." The lie was getting easier by the second. "We danced and danced. Ryan couldn't keep his hands off me."

Because if he'd let go, he'd have dropped straight to the floor, Jessica added bitterly to herself, but the smile she'd plastered to her face never wavered.

Jessica felt bad about misleading her friend, especially after Miranda had been so supportive through all her troubles with Ben and Priya, but she just couldn't bring herself to tell her the truth. It was too pathetic. The whole beach didn't need to know what a loser Ryan had been the night before—how she'd pushed his drunken butt right out onto the pavement. And no one—absolutely no one—needed to know how thoroughly Ryan had humiliated her by calling her Elizabeth. No, Jessica planned to carry that little secret all the way to her grave.

"Wow. You're so lucky." Miranda sighed enviously.

Yeah. About as lucky as a broken mirror, Jessica thought, wondering what she was going to do about Ryan. There was no way she wanted to spend another evening with him like the one she'd endured the night before. But on the other hand, she couldn't very well dump him either. Elizabeth would say "I told you so," of course, but that was the least of it. Jessica was a lot more worried about what Ben and Priya would say.

She could practically hear it already. "Some women just can't hold on to a man," Priya would smirk, fawning all over Ben. "I guess after a couple of days the thrill of a perfect tan wears off, then a guy expects you to be able to actually *think*."

Jessica's eyes narrowed angrily at the imagined insult. Just thinking about Priya made Jessica want to hit something—hard. She'd never met anyone so good at making her feel so bad. Not to mention the fact that Priya had stolen Ben right out from under her. No, Jessica couldn't fail so soon at her relationship with Ryan. If she did, she'd never hear the end of it.

"So are you going to see Ryan again tonight?" Miranda asked, interrupting her thoughts.

"Maybe not tonight . . ." Jessica stalled, suddenly worried if she was ever going to see him again. After all, she hadn't been very under-standing—or forgiving—the night before. What if he didn't want to see *her* now?

"Hey, Jessica," a familiar voice called up from the sand, as if on cue. "Hey, I'm really sorry."

Jessica looked down from the tower rail, appalled to see Ryan standing directly beneath her. Gulping, she glanced over at Miranda. Obviously if Jessica's glowing reports about the night before were true, then Ryan had nothing to apologize for.

"Sorry about what, sweetie?" Jessica asked nervously, trying to keep her voice light for Miranda's benefit. Meanwhile she was hurrying down the tower stairs as fast as she could go. She had to get Ryan away from Miranda!

"You know. About last night," Ryan replied before she could reach him.

Jessica flinched, hoping that by some miracle Miranda hadn't heard him. She grabbed Ryan by the arm, hustling him down the beach away from the tower.

"Look, I know I was a total jerk last night," Ryan apologized as they walked. "I can't tell you how embarrassed I am about it."

"You *were* a jerk," Jessica agreed coolly. "But are you sure you wouldn't rather be talking to my sister? You know, *Elizabeth*?"

Ryan winced. "Look, Jess, that's the most embarrassing part of the whole thing. I was

130

drunk, that's all. Give me another chance," he begged. "I promise I'll make it up to you."

"I don't know . . . ," Jessica said slowly. But she did, of course. Another date with Ryan was already a done deal.

"Then I'll have to convince you," Ryan said, an easy smile on his lips.

The next thing Jessica knew, Ryan had swept her into his arms and was kissing her the way that only Ryan could. At first she resisted, but gradually she melted up against him, returning his kisses eagerly. This wasn't the disgusting Ryan of the night before—this Ryan was showered and sober. Best of all, he was totally gorgeous and completely hers.

"So what's on the agenda for tonight?" Jessica asked when she could catch her breath. "And don't you dare say Louie's Liquor Lounge."

Ryan looked genuinely embarrassed. "I really *am* sorry about last night, Jessica. I'll never wreck a date that way again."

"Hmmm . . ."

"How about a romantic dinner at my place? Just the two of us?" Ryan suggested. "I'll call out for Chinese food, and we'll turn the lights down low. . . ."

Jessica let him dangle a moment. "I suppose I could clear my schedule," she finally allowed.

"Great!" Ryan exclaimed. "It's a date, then." He kissed her briefly one last time. "See you at seven?"

"Seven," Jessica agreed, barely able to keep the canary-eating smile off her face as Ryan walked back up the beach toward the Main Tower.

Phew, that was close, she thought, climbing the stairs to the tower platform. But everything had worked out great. She and Ryan were back together, for better or for worse.

"What was that all about?" Miranda asked curiously as Jessica resumed her position beside her at the rail. "Why was Ryan apologizing for last night?"

"What?" Jessica replied, startled. "Oh, that! He was just sorry that the night had to end so *soon,*" she covered, relieved that her earlier lies hadn't been exposed. "Not to worry, though. We're having dinner at his place tonight."

And only *dinner,* she told herself emphatically. *Drinks are strictly out. Still, it shouldn't be too hard to keep Ryan's hands off the bottle when he can be wrapping them around me instead.*

"Wow. You're so lucky," Miranda repeated, sighing.

Luckier than you know, Jessica thought, breathing a silent sigh of relief.

"What's ringing?" Nina asked, her expression half confused and half annoyed. "Elizabeth, what's that noise?"

It was getting late, almost quitting time, but Elizabeth thought Nina seemed even more keyed up than she'd been at the beginning of their shift. "It sounds like the emergency telephone," she answered, hurrying from the platform into the glassed-in part of the Main Tower. "I'll get it."

Inside the tower the ringing was loud and clear. Elizabeth rushed to answer the old-fashioned black telephone, the one kept strictly for emergencies. In all her time as a lifeguard Elizabeth had only heard the emergency phone ring twice before. Her hand trembled as she brought the handset to her ear. "Main Tower."

"Uh . . . yeah . . . hi," the caller stuttered on the other end of the line. "Can I talk to Ryan?"

"Ryan's not here right now," Elizabeth replied, not wanting to explain to a stranger that he'd quit. "If there's an emergency, I can help you."

"No. Uh, I need to talk to Ryan," the caller insisted stubbornly. "Is he coming right back?"

"Not exactly." Elizabeth chewed her lip nervously, then made a decision. "I can let you speak to Nina Harper. She's the new squad leader." Elizabeth was walking as she spoke. She reeled out yard after yard of the long phone cord as she made her way out to the platform and Nina's side.

"No! Um . . . I mean . . . that's no good." The man on the phone was beginning to sound panicked. "I need to speak to Ryan!" Elizabeth made a helpless gesture at Nina and covered the mouthpiece with one hand. "He only wants Ryan," she mouthed.

Nina grabbed the phone away. "This is an emergency line, sir," she said briskly. "My name is Nina Harper, and I'm in charge here. Please state the nature of your emergency, or I'll have to disconnect the call."

There was a pause as Nina listened to the caller. "I can't spare a lifeguard to track Ryan down for a personal call . . . ," she began, then stopped to listen again. "A personal emergency?" She listened a while longer, shaking her head impatiently. "OK, stand by."

"What's going on?" Elizabeth whispered to Nina. "Who is that?"

"I don't know, but the guy's freaking out," Nina replied, her hand over the mouthpiece. "He's crying, and he says he has to talk to Ryan. Some type of personal emergency. Listen, Liz, go downstairs and see if he's in his room."

"Nina!" Elizabeth protested. "I don't want to talk to him!"

"Just do it, OK?" Nina snapped. There were bags under her deep brown eyes, and she sounded exhausted. "Be the bigger person for once."

Be the bigger person for once! I'm always the bigger person. The unfair accusation rankled as Elizabeth trotted angrily down the outside stairs to Ryan's room. She rapped at Ryan's door, then shouted through it impatiently. "Ryan! Telephone!"

A moment later Ryan appeared. "What?" he asked, a tentative smile on his face. He looked amazed to see her, but pleasantly so.

"You have a call on the emergency telephone. Nina's got it up on the platform."

Ryan drew his eyebrows together, his expression confused. "Why doesn't she take the call? I'm not on the squad anymore."

"I don't know, Ryan!" Elizabeth snapped, annoyed at being the messenger girl. Especially when Ryan looked so cute. And happy to see her. And sober.

For a moment Elizabeth allowed herself to imagine pushing Ryan backward into his room and throwing herself into his arms. He'd kiss her, he'd want her back—Elizabeth was sure of it. But everything was so complicated now. Ryan wasn't her serious, responsible boss anymore. He was the alcoholic waste case dating her backstabbing sister.

Meanwhile there was an emergency phone call waiting. "Listen, you'd better come up," she told Ryan. "Nina says the guy on the phone is crying. Some kind of personal emergency, he says."

"Crying?" Ryan's eyes reflected his alarm. "Who is it?"

Elizabeth would have answered that she had no idea, but Ryan was already sprinting up the tower stairs, taking them two at a time. By the time Elizabeth got upstairs, Ryan was speaking urgently into the telephone.

"Arthur! Arthur, what's . . . I can't understand you. Try to calm down."

135

Elizabeth raised her eyebrows at Nina, but Nina only shrugged. She didn't know what was going on either.

"Arthur, you have to calm down," Ryan repeated. "Now tell me what happened."

Elizabeth's hand flew up to her mouth as she suddenly realized who Ryan was talking to. It was Arthur Yager, Patti's husband. And Patti was off the wagon.

What if there's been an accident? Elizabeth worried, trying to catch Ryan's eye for some type of clue. But Ryan wouldn't look at her. The hand he held the phone with shook as he listened to his former A.A. sponsor's husband while the other one groped blindly behind him for the railing.

"OK," Ryan said. His voice sounded choked and unsteady, barely under control. "OK, you too." He hung up the phone.

"Ryan, what is it?" Elizabeth cried. "What happened?"

But Ryan didn't answer. Instead he turned around and hurried down the tower stairs.

Elizabeth exchanged a quick, anxious look with Nina, then ran after Ryan. "Ryan! Please tell me what's going on," she pleaded. They reached the bottom of the stairs, then Ryan's door. "Ryan! Please!"

Ryan turned around, one hand on the doorknob, and his expression took Elizabeth's breath away. Every plane of his face seemed frozen in place. His usually warm brown eyes were cold and lifeless.

"Ryan! What's happened?"

"I don't want to talk about it," he said. Then he rushed into his room and slammed the door in Elizabeth's face.

Elizabeth stood there, stunned. It was always the same with Ryan. He *always* shut her out, one way or another.

"So what else is new?" she shouted through the door, her voice full of hurt and frustration. "You never want to talk about anything!"

Her only reply was complete and total silence.

Chapter Nine

"Ryan! Ryan, please, what's wrong?"

Ryan could hear Elizabeth pounding on his locked door, but he didn't care. It was getting so hard to care about anything anymore. In a lot of ways this latest news wasn't even a shock. He was starting to think that if you wanted something bad to happen, all you had to do was wait.

"Patti's in the hospital." Arthur Yager's voice echoed in his head as clearly as if he were still on the telephone. *"She'd been drinking, and she . . . she ran the car into a wall. She's on life support, Ryan. They . . . I . . . I don't know if she's going to make it."* At that, Patti's husband had broken down in hysterics. Ryan clenched his fists over his ears, trying to block out the horrible memory of Arthur's sobs.

"Ryan! Ryan, let me in!" Elizabeth demanded loudly from outside.

"It's my fault," Arthur's voice resounded in Ryan's head. *"I shouldn't have let her take the car. I should have found a way to stop her. . . ."*

"Ryan, don't do this! I want to help you!"

"She just . . . she seemed like she could handle it. I didn't know how drunk she was. I thought she'd come around."

"Ryan—"

"Shut up!" Ryan screamed, the words ripped from his throat as if his voice belonged to someone else. "Shut up, both of you! Just leave me alone!"

The pounding on his door ceased abruptly. The voice in his head receded.

"Leave me alone," he repeated miserably, throwing himself facedown on the couch and clasping a pillow over his head.

What did people expect from him? Didn't they see he was barely holding on as it was? He had enough on his mind without Elizabeth and her constant, inflexible demands, without Arthur's inconsolable grief over Patti.

Oh no. Patti. Ryan didn't even want to think about Patti in the hospital, machines pumping air into her lungs and fluids into her veins. But it was better than imagining her in the car wreck. Arthur said she'd hit a concrete freeway wall head-on. At full speed. Almost as if she'd intended to do it . . .

No, it was an accident! Ryan chastised himself. *It had to have been an accident.*

He wondered if the accident had been very bloody, if Patti would ever fully recover. But he already knew that it had to have been horrible. In his mind's eye Ryan saw shattered windows, twisted metal, and gasoline pooling on the pavement.

And the pain. *It must have hurt. It must have hurt so bad.* . . . He envisioned his own body flying through the windshield, glass blowing like a blizzard, and the bone-crushing impact as he slammed into the wall.

"Aaaaugh!" he shouted, throwing the pillow off his head. He couldn't think about it anymore. He couldn't think about anything anymore.

Running to the counter where he'd left the whiskey, Ryan seized the bottle. His right hand trembled uncontrollably as he wrestled with the cap. He'd get enough whiskey inside him to forget it all—that was his plan. He'd forget Elizabeth and how disappointed in him she was, he'd forget how he'd thrown away the only career he'd ever cared about, and he'd forget—he'd *definitely* forget—the fact that Patti was lying in intensive care somewhere, barely clinging to life.

The first swallow burned down his throat, snapping him back to his senses. *Drinking won't fix this,* warned a voice inside his head. *You ought to go visit Patti.*

"Patti won't even know you're there!" he shouted back savagely. "And you're a fool if you think you can fix *anything,* Ryan Taylor."

He lifted the bottle higher, swallowing as fast as he could.

"You honestly make the best vegetable soup I've ever tasted, Stu," Nina said, putting down her spoon.

Stu smiled at her from across the giant bowl they shared. "I didn't think you ate enough to taste it."

"I'm sorry." Nina shrugged apologetically. "I'm just so wound up. I'm not very hungry."

"You didn't eat any breakfast either," Stu reminded her gently, shaking his soup spoon for emphasis. "Starving yourself won't fix anything. Come on, eat a little more."

Nina picked up her spoon reluctantly, a forced smile on her lips. "I'll try."

The two of them were sitting cross-legged on the floor in Stu's meditation room, with the soup in between them on a small wooden table. The sun had just begun setting on the beach outside the large round window, and everything about the island was beautiful, peaceful, serene.

But Nina couldn't relax. She kept imagining Rachel in this very same house the night before, trying to trick Stu into marrying her. Or—even worse—Rachel sneaking into Nina's room at the beach house, intent on revenge. How crazy was Rachel, really? Was she . . . could she be . . . crazy enough to kill someone?

"In order to eat, you have to actually put the spoon in the bowl and then in your mouth," Stu said, slipping his arms around her from behind. Nina had been so preoccupied with her thoughts that she hadn't even noticed he'd moved.

"I'm sorry," she apologized again. "I just can't. It *was* good, though."

Stu held her gently, rocking her back and forth. "You know what would calm your nerves? Herbal tea. I've got this new one from Tibet that's absolutely killer. You want me to make you some?"

"I don't think tea's the answer, Stu. A straitjacket might do it—buckled around the right psycho, of course."

"You can't let Rachel get to you like this. I admit she's kind of scary, but what if we're totally overreacting? She's probably harmless."

Nina snorted with disbelief. "Harmless, Stu? The woman's a mental case! Or have you forgotten she wanted to turn this room into the nursery for a baby she's not even having?"

"No. And why did she have to pick *this* room?" Stu complained, suddenly annoyed. "It's not like a baby knows the difference. Meanwhile, this is *my* favorite room."

"Stu! There is *no baby!*" Nina shouted, all the tension of the previous two days venting itself in her voice.

Stu stiffened with surprise, and even Nina

was shocked by her outburst. "Wow, I'm sorry," she apologized sheepishly. "I . . . I don't know what's wrong with me. I'm just . . . scared, I guess. That's all."

Stu's arms folded her tighter, reassuring her. "I'm so sorry I got you mixed up in this. I'd do anything to keep you out of it. But you're safe here, I promise."

Nina leaned back into the safety of Stu's embrace. "I don't know which of us is in more danger at this point," she joked weakly. "Rachel probably wants to murder me—but she wants to *marry* you."

Stu chuckled. "I'll get you out of this," he vowed. "Don't worry."

"You're darn right you will. That's what karma's all about, right?"

"Well, something like that," Stu agreed, kissing the top of her head. "I must have really messed up in a past life to deserve this, though." He paused. "You know what? I'm going to go make that tea after all. I think it'll help."

"No, Stu," Nina protested. "I'd rather have you stay right where you are." She wriggled around to face him, wrapping her arms around his neck and kissing him tenderly. "Mmmmm. This is a lot more calming than tea."

"There's no reason you can't have both," Stu replied, smiling as he disentangled himself. "Come on, we could both use some. I'll go make it, and I'll be right back."

"Stu . . ."

But he was already gone, swallowed up somewhere between Nina and the kitchen in that enormous house of his.

"Great," Nina muttered, getting up and wandering toward the window. The last thing she wanted right now was a cup of tea. A prescription tranquilizer for her, a restraining order for Rachel—something like that might have helped. But what good was tea going to do?

Try to get a grip, Nina told herself, barely seeing the spectacular sunset outside. *Stu's right— you need to calm down.*

She focused on her breathing, trying to remember what Stu had taught her about concentrating her energies. The sun was an explosion of orange on the horizon, stains of pink and purple seeping across the clouds. Nina modulated her breathing, her eyes on all that natural beauty. Gradually she felt calmer, more in control of her emotions. Maybe she'd even be able to drink whatever way-too-natural concoction Stu was brewing in the kitchen.

The thought made Nina smile. Stu was the best thing that had ever happened to her. If she spent enough time on SeaMist Island, Nina could actually imagine herself being calm all the time, not to mention completely, totally happy.

She stepped back from the window and glanced at the room around her. A meditation room! It was so Stu. No one else Nina knew would even think of meditating, let alone building a special room for it. But it *was* a peaceful room. There was hardly any furniture in the pale blue octagon—only Stu's meditation mat with the matching pillow, a couple of small tables, and the one long, benchlike table that hugged the window wall of the room. It was there that Stu placed his treasures: a special shell, a red glass bottle that lit like a ruby in the sun, polished sea stones, an intricate metal sculpture. . . .

Hey, wait a minute! Nina told herself. *What happened to the sculpture?*

Nina backed up, confused. There was no way Stu would have gotten rid of that sculpture. It was his favorite thing in the room. *So where is it?* she wondered, strangely worried.

"Looking for *this?*"

Nina whirled around to see Rachel standing right behind her, the heavy, angular sculpture raised over her head to strike.

"Stu!" Nina screamed, her heart in her throat. But it was too late. The sculpture was already on its way down.

"This place is unbelievable," Wendy breathed, pulling her Mercedes up to the front of the Sweet Valley Ocean Palace. Uniformed valets immediately rushed to open the car doors, then whisked the Mercedes away as Wendy and

Winston walked into the open, Hawaiian-style lobby. The Pacific Ocean glittered in the setting sun in front of them.

"I told you," Winston crowed, hustling Wendy confidently through the lobby.

"What I want to know is how much this little excursion is going to cost me," Wendy countered skeptically. "The guy must be loaded if he's staying here."

"Don't worry about it," Winston said as they came to Pedro's suite. "I've got it covered."

"*You* do?" Wendy's eyebrows shot up in surprise. "What did you do, Winston? Promise him your firstborn son?"

"Very funny," Winston said calmly. "Look, here's the door. Go ahead and knock, then walk right in."

"Don't worry. I'll be right behind you."

"No, Wendy," Winston protested. "I don't think I ought to go in with you. This is so private and—"

"Bull," Wendy interrupted. "You've been in to see every other crackpot you made me go to. I'm not about to let you off the hook now that we're here to meet their king."

"Wendy!"

But it was no use. Wendy knocked and deftly pushed the door open with one hand. Then, with a quick shove of the other, she propelled Winston into the room ahead of her.

146

"Wow!" Winston heard Wendy gasp as they walked into the living room.

Yeah, wow, Winston echoed silently. He had timed their entrance perfectly. The setting sun was framed like a jewel in the open French doors. The silk on the walls shimmered with the softest of sea breezes, while the flickering white candles lent an ethereal glow to the entire scene. Winston detected the scents of salt air and sandalwood incense as he faltered forward into the suite, almost as impressed as Wendy.

"Uh, G-Guru Futi," he stuttered, stumbling over his lines. "This is, uh, Wendy Paloma. She wishes to consult Your, um, Majesticness."

Majesticness! Egbert, you idiot! Winston berated himself as he walked the rest of the way into the room. *You sound like a total moron!*

Surprisingly, though, Pedro really *did* look majestic—incredibly so. His goatee was gone at last, and the wig and false mustache were carefully in place. Pedro's white suit gleamed in the failing light, and something about his tired brown eyes looked old and wise. He sat regally in the high-backed chair, gesturing for Wendy to take the seat facing him. The glass table that had been between the chairs the night before was gone, Winston noted. Apparently Pedro had decided against trying to use the crystals.

It's just as well, Winston thought distractedly, hoping Pedro would be able to pull the whole thing off.

147

"What is it you seek, my child?" Pedro asked as Wendy stepped forward and slipped eagerly into the chair across from his.

Winston's body went slack with relief. Pedro's delivery was dead convincing. He watched the awestruck expression on Wendy's face with mixed satisfaction and pride as she leaned forward, straining toward her new guru.

"Guru Futi," she began, her voice hushed and reverent. "I've come about my husband. I married too young and too quickly, and to a man who's never around. I want to be out of that relationship."

Ouch! Winston thought, sinking into a cross-legged position in the farthest corner of the room. *She's not pulling any punches.* His heart sank as he worried whether Pedro would be able to take it, if he'd be able to hear what Wendy had to say and still stay in character.

"This husband," Pedro began. "Has he mistreated you? Does he no longer love you?"

Wendy waved one hand impatiently. "That's not the point, Guru Futi. My husband is never *here.* That's no kind of marriage."

Pedro closed his eyes and made a steeple of his fingers. Winston suspected that the singer was simply trying to regain his cool, but Wendy seemed convinced that the "guru" was thinking deep thoughts.

She's totally buying it, Winston realized. *Heck, I'm practically buying it.*

"This husband, do you love him?" Pedro asked after a lengthy pause.

"It's . . . I . . . that doesn't matter anymore," Wendy stammered. "It's too late."

"Too late for what, my child?"

"For us! For me and Pedro. Isn't that what you see too, Guru Futi?"

Pedro furrowed his false silver brows, concentrating intensely. Wendy leaned farther forward in her chair, her eyes glued to his.

"I do not receive an insight with regard to your marriage," he said at last.

Wendy looked crushed.

"But then, foreseeing the future is not my specialty," the guru added quickly. "I am known around the world for my psychic channeling abilities. Perhaps we may seek an insight that way?"

Wendy, so disappointed a second before, brightened instantly. "Do you think it would help?"

Pedro smiled kindly. "One can only try. What would you have me channel to this husband, this Pedro?"

"What do you mean?"

"What is it that you wish him to know?"

"That's easy. Tell him that we're through. That it's over between us."

"I will tell him what you—"

"Oh yeah! And tell him I'm in love with Winston Egbert now. He might as well know that too."

Pedro winced visibly.

Uh-oh, Winston thought as Pedro began to shudder uncontrollably, his eyes squeezed tightly shut. *She went too far. He's going to blow his cover. Maybe I should run while I still have the chance.*

But Wendy was clearly enthralled. "Guru Futi, what is it?" she cried. "Are you speaking to Pedro?"

"Please!" Pedro held up a hand for silence. His trembling continued, becoming increasingly more violent, until Winston actually started to worry that his friend was having a seizure. He was trying to decide if he ought to call for help when suddenly Pedro jerked bolt upright, as if an electric shock had just exploded through his body. His eyes flew open, wide and unseeing, and a strangled cry escaped his lips.

Winston leaped to his feet in a panic. "Pedro!" he shouted. But before he could cross the room, Wendy jumped from her chair and dropped onto her knees, grabbing her guru's hands in hers.

"Yes! Pedro!" she repeated urgently. "Please, Guru Futi. What does Pedro have to say to me?"

Chapter
Ten

Wait till Ryan gets a load of this *new outfit,* Jessica congratulated herself, smoothing the fabric of her tight black minidress over her hips. *He won't be thinking about drinking, that's for sure.*

But in the unlikely event that the dress didn't hold Ryan's complete attention, Jessica was prepared. The basket over her arm held her other tricks: an expensive box of chocolates to share, a bottle of sparkling cider, a homemade cassette tape of the most romantic songs she knew, and her sexiest black bikini.

You've met your match tonight, Ryan Taylor, she thought with a satisfied smile as she knocked confidently on the door of Ryan's tower bedroom. She could already imagine how the evening would go. First they'd have the Chinese food Ryan had promised, then maybe some cider and chocolates. After that they'd dance to the steamy ballads on the tape Jessica had made. Later, when things got too hot, they'd change into their suits for a romantic, moonlit swim. . . .

All this assuming that Ryan answered the door, of course. What was keeping him?

"Ryan?" Jessica called, knocking again and pressing her ear against the wood to listen.

The door opened suddenly and with such a jerk that Jessica lost her balance and stumbled into the room. She fell right into Ryan, her hands bracing against his chest to keep her from going down.

"Jessica!" Ryan exclaimed. The alcohol on his breath almost knocked her out. "What are you doing here?"

"What am I doing here?" she repeated indignantly, pushing him away. "We had a date, remember?"

"We did?" Ryan's eyes were glassy and unfocused, and he swayed where he stood. The sunset had barely faded from the sky, but it was clear that her Romeo was already plastered.

"You're drunk!" Jessica accused furiously.

Ryan laughed—a harsh, raucous sound. "D'ya think?" he asked, just barely slurring. "What tipped you off?"

"That's it," Jessica spat. "You promised you wouldn't drink tonight. I've been pretty understanding up till now, Ryan, but this—"

"Yeah, yeah," Ryan interrupted, stripping the

152

basket off her arm and dropping it to the floor. "Fascinating. But now we have to go." He grabbed her by the arm and pulled her out into the darkness, slamming the tower door behind them.

"Ryan!" she protested. "Let go of me! What are you doing?"

"No time to talk, Jess. Come on!" There was a wild look in Ryan's eyes as he dragged her across the dry sand north of the Main Tower.

"Stop it! Where are we going?"

"You'll see," he promised. "Something happened today—something that made it all make sense."

"Made *what* make sense?" Jessica demanded, wresting her arm out of his grip. "I'm not going anywhere with you until you tell me what's going on."

Ryan's smile was shallow, noncommittal. "Whatever. It doesn't matter, don't you see? That's the key. *Nothing matters.*"

Jessica glared at him, her hands on her hips. Not only had Ryan totally let her down, but she was also getting sick of his cryptic nonsense. "That's the biggest load I've ever heard," she told him angrily. "I'm going home."

Ryan shrugged. "Whatever," he said again. Then he turned and started running up the sand.

"Ryan Taylor! Where are you going?" Jessica shouted at his back. She could absolutely kill him! How *dare* he not care if she stayed or went? And where was he going anyway? There was nothing north of the Main Tower except the harbor, and the Sweet Valley Shore Harbor wasn't much to see. Just a few old fishing boats and the Harbor Patrol vessels. The lifeguards spent a couple of days each summer training on the Harbor Patrol's small rescue boats, but they never actually *used* them. That was the Harbor Patrol's job.

Suddenly a small, cold knot formed in Jessica's stomach. Ryan couldn't be thinking about taking a rescue boat out joyriding. Could he? It was already almost completely dark, and Ryan was drunk as a skunk.

"He'll be killed!" Jessica gasped, fear blossoming inside her. "I can't let him do it!"

Kicking off her high heels and picking them up in one hand, Jessica took off running after Ryan. The cool, dry sand slowed her progress, but Jessica ran on determinedly. She had to catch Ryan before he did something stupid!

Unfortunately Ryan had a head start and longer legs. Even intoxicated, he sprinted across the sand as if it were the easiest thing in the world. Jessica could no longer see him in the darkness ahead of her. She reached the jetty and scrambled up the riprap, hoping she wasn't already too late.

"Ryan!"

She spotted him on the main dock, fiddling

around with a rescue boat exactly as Jessica had feared. A pool of light from one of the lamps spaced along the old wooden jetty illuminated his face as he turned in the direction of her voice.

"Jessica!" he called back, obviously surprised but happy to see her. "You changed your mind."

"Uh, yeah," Jessica lied. "Wait for me, OK?"

Ryan waved agreement and turned back toward the boat. Hurriedly Jessica made her way down the other side of the jetty, then sprinted across the packed dirt and concrete to the dock. The speedboat's engine roared to life. Jessica ran up alongside it and stopped, clutching her sides and gasping for breath.

"Get in," Ryan commanded. He was already standing in the boat, holding impatiently in one hand the single line that kept the boat tethered to the dock. "Let's go."

He reached out his other hand to her, but Jessica backed away. "I can't let you do this," she told him. "It's crazy. You could get killed."

"What?" Ryan seemed confused for a moment, then his face clouded angrily. "If you didn't want to ride, why did you make me wait for you?"

"It's too dangerous, Ryan," Jessica pleaded urgently, genuinely worried. "Please don't do this. Listen to me. I want to help you."

"Oh, of *course!* You want to *help* me!" Ryan snorted, his voice thick with alcohol and sarcasm. "I should have known that you and your

155

killjoy sister were total clones after all."

Jessica bristled.

"You know what would help me?" he taunted. "You know what would help me a lot, in fact? If you, and Elizabeth, and Arthur, and all the rest of the do-gooders in the world would just leave me the hell alone!"

"That's fine with me!" Jessica retorted, spinning around on the dock and stalking off. "If I never see you again, it'll be too soon!"

She had only taken a couple of angry steps, though, when Ryan grabbed her from behind and lifted her up off her feet. "Where ya goin', beautiful?" he asked, carrying her back toward the boat. "I thought we were taking a cruise."

"Stop it!" she screamed, dropping her best black heels on the dock in her struggle to get away. "Let go of me, Ryan!"

"Nah. I don't think so."

Jessica's spine tingled with fear when she realized they were at the boat again—and Ryan was lowering her into it.

"Ryan, stop it!" she demanded, kicking her feet.

But it was no use; Ryan was too strong. He dropped her the rest of the way, her sudden weight rocking the speedboat crazily. Before Jessica could recover, Ryan untied the boat and pushed it off from the dock, leaping in beside her at the same time. The boat pitched and rolled but leveled quickly, shooting away from the dock as Ryan hit the throttle. The sudden acceleration threw Jessica over backward. She landed hard on the bottom of the boat, her tight black minidress hiking up indecently.

"You're dead!" she screamed at Ryan from her undignified position. "If Captain Feehan doesn't kill you for this, I will!"

"Yeah, sure. Save it for someone who's listening," Ryan tossed back over his shoulder as he steered the speeding boat in a wide, slipshod arc out of the harbor and into the open ocean.

Even in the darkness Jessica could tell they were going much, much faster than she'd ever gone in one of the rescue boats before. The motor whined, and the hull slapped the tops of the swells, just skimming across the water. Gripping the gunwales, Jessica pulled herself up onto her feet, looking back in the direction of the harbor as a chill wind whipped her hair around her face. Already the dock lights had receded into little pinpricks and the harbor was falling away off their stern like a mirage. A sick, hollow fear gripped her as she realized she was alone on the ocean with a drunken, out-of-control lunatic.

"Help!" she screamed vainly back toward shore. "Somebody help me!"

"I thought you were here to help *me*, babe." Ryan laughed from the steering console. "Where's all that goodwill when I need it?"

"You shut up!" she screeched, wondering if she

157

dared try to swim for it. But it was too far, too dark.

"Help!" Jessica screamed again, knowing there was no chance in the world that anyone would hear her.

"Aaah!" Rachel shrieked, bringing the sculpture down with all her strength. The heavy metal structure swung easily in her hands, speeding down toward its target. It would crack Nina's head like a nut! But at the last second Nina dodged and the sculpture missed its mark, crashing noisily to the floor instead.

"Stu!" Nina bleated like the pathetic little sheep she was. "Stu, help!"

"Oh, please," Rachel sneered, keeping her body between Nina and the doorway to prevent an escape. "You really *do* think I'm stupid. Stuart's *mine*, not yours. And anyway, he's not in any position to help you right now."

Nina's eyes went wide with panic. "What have you done to Stu?" she demanded. "If you hurt him, I swear I'll—"

"*Hurt* him?" Rachel cut her off. "What's wrong with you? Stuart's my world. *You're* the one I'm going to hurt."

Nina froze in place. Rachel edged forward slowly, her muscles tensed to spring. She could hear pounding from across the house now. *Stuart's trying to get out of the bathroom,* she realized, feeling her time running out. Rachel had kept hidden until Stuart had gone into the half bath nearest the kitchen, then she'd pushed a chair against the outside doorknob to keep him from escaping. Judging by the noise he was making, though, it wouldn't be long before he kicked his way out. *By the time he does, my job will be finished,* she thought with wicked glee.

"Why are you doing this?" Nina asked suddenly, her expression shifting from fear to anger. "Don't you know you can't win? Stu doesn't love you. You're not even having his baby!"

"How *dare* you!" Rachel screamed, lunging to attack. "I *hate* you!" Her hands closed around Nina's neck, and with a tremendous, twisting shove, Rachel forced her rival to the ground. "You'd better say your prayers, girl," she grunted as her hands tightened down on Nina's throat, squeezing, squeezing.

But Nina kicked wildly, thrashing under Rachel's weight. "Let go of me, you psycho!" she cried, gouging at Rachel's wrists with her fingernails.

Nina's nails bit deeply, and Rachel felt the warm, sticky sensation of her own blood running down her hands. She sucked in her breath, watching as the red stain blossomed across her skin. It was right that there be blood. It was fitting. It wasn't important that the blood was her own.

The blood will wash me clean, she thought, smiling as she rocked back and forth. *The blood will take the guilt.*

159

It was a sign. A sign from David.

Rachel increased her grip on Nina's neck, confident now that she was doing the right thing. "I can't believe you thought you'd get away with it," she told Nina in a confidential tone. "I mean, since you're dying now, I guess I can say that. First you took my boyfriend, and then you stole my picture! Did you think I'd let that slide? You were trying to take my *life*."

"You're crazy!" Nina shot back. Then with a tremendous, unexpected kick, she broke free, struggling up onto her knees.

But Rachel recovered before Nina could regain her feet. Shoving her viciously from behind, Rachel sent Nina sprawling again, this time facedown on Stuart's meditation mat.

"Now I've got you," Rachel cried, springing onto Nina's prone back. Fast as thought, she clamped the meditation pillow down over Nina's head, smothering her against the mat.

"You thought you could take my life," Rachel whispered, holding on in spite of Nina's frantic struggles. "But now the tables are turned, aren't they?" Rachel bore down with the pillow, willing the air out of Nina's body. Everything would be OK again if Nina would just stop breathing. Rachel and Stuart would be reunited, baby David would be born on his father's island, and someday this whole unappealing episode would fade from all their memories.

If anything, Stuart would be embarrassed by the way he'd cheated on her.

"Stop kicking!" Rachel urged through the pillow as Nina's struggles became more feeble. "Stop *breathing!*"

She could still hear Stuart pounding away on the bathroom door. Or was that only the blood pounding in her ears? Rachel wasn't certain anymore. All she knew for sure was that she was on her way. The last thing standing between her and happiness was Nina Harper. And Nina was never going to stand again. Rachel was seeing to that.

Gradually Nina's feet stopped moving, and her back stopped heaving. And then she was still. So still.

Watch out. She could be faking, Rachel cautioned herself, still bearing down on the pillow. *There's no hurry now. Make sure she's good and dead.* Rachel lost track of the moments that passed as she lay there on Nina's back, a determined grip on Stuart's meditation pillow.

"Ray-Ray?"

The faltering voice behind her was soft, uncertain. Rachel's heart froze at the sound, and her breath caught in her chest. She hesitated, afraid to turn around, afraid to even hope. How many times before had she heard that precious voice, only to have it fade off into a dream?

"Ray-Ray, it's me, David."

"David?" Rachel echoed. She lifted her head

slowly, praying the voice was real this time. "David, where are you?"

"I'm right here. Turn around."

Trembling with longing, Rachel let go of the pillow and rose from Nina's still body. Then she turned, and her buckling knees almost gave out beneath her. He was here! He was real! The young man standing in front of her was tall and beautiful. His strong arms reached out to hold her.

"Oh, David. Is it really you?" she gasped. It looked like David, but how would she know? How could she be sure after so many years?

"Of course it's me. It's so good to see you, Rachel. Come give me a hug."

Rachel stumbled toward him awkwardly, then rushed into his arms, overcome as they wrapped around her and encircled her with warmth. "Oh, David!" she sobbed, burying her face against his chest. "It's really you. It's really you! Where have you been?"

"What have you done to Nina?" David asked gently, pushing her out to arm's length and looking into her face. His eyes were blue—bluer than the sky. Bluer than she remembered.

"Who? Oh, her. She's dead. David, take me away from here. Something happened. . . . I thought you were someone . . . I . . . oh, David, why were you gone so *long?*" Rachel's entire body shook with the emotion of seeing him again. "Why did—"

But David suddenly threw her to one side, dropping to his knees next to her prey. He removed the pillow from its head and carefully, tenderly turned the lifeless body onto its back, feeling for a pulse in the neck.

Why does David care? Rachel wondered, stunned. *Sure, Stuart thought he liked that girl, but he was wrong. Anyway, now that David's back, I couldn't care less what Stuart—*

Rachel sucked in her breath as reality suddenly washed over her with the unwelcome brilliance of an atomic blast. The man on his knees wasn't David after all. It was *Stuart!* It was *Stuart* bending over her prey's motionless face, showering it with tears. It was *Stuart* who had tricked Rachel into letting go of the pillow.

It was *Stuart* pretending to be the most longed-for love of her life.

"David!" Rachel shrieked, the sound echoing off the bare walls. "No! I want David!" The pain seared so intensely, it felt like an animal clawing through her.

But David wasn't there. He'd *never* been there. And Stuart didn't love her. She wasn't having his baby. The sobs rose up to choke her, making her retch with dry heaves.

"Oh, David. Why did you have to leave me?" she cried.

* * *

"Someone's having a wild night," Elizabeth muttered, peering out her bedroom window toward the beach. It was too dark to see the water, but she could hear the sound of a whining speedboat tearing up the ocean out past the surf line. Even though she couldn't see the boat, Elizabeth could tell by the way the engine was laboring that it was being driven way too fast, especially considering the fact that the driver wouldn't be able to see the water in front of him. "He won't think it's so fun if Captain Feehan catches him," Elizabeth added darkly, turning from the window. If the local sheriff sent out the Harbor Patrol, the driver would be cited for reckless driving.

Disgusted, Elizabeth crossed the room and threw herself down on her single bed. The beach house was deathly quiet. Nina was over at Stu's place, and Jessica had gone to Miranda's condo. Ben was downstairs somewhere, but Elizabeth didn't hang out with Ben very often. Besides, he was almost certainly with Priya.

No, Elizabeth was on her own, with nothing better to do than obsess about Ryan. She was still mad at him for telling her to shut up, of course, but more than that she was worried. Something horrible must have happened to Patti to make Ryan act the way he had. As soon as she'd gotten home from the beach, even before she'd changed out of her bathing suit and into her blue sweats, Elizabeth had made calls to all three hospitals in the Sweet Valley Shore area, fishing for information about Patti. But no one would tell her anything. She still wasn't sure Patti was even *in* a hospital.

"Some Friday night," she grumbled, thinking she must be the most pathetic person in all of California.

At least Jessica went over to Miranda's instead of to Ryan's, she consoled herself. Elizabeth had been pretty surprised by her sister's choice, but she'd been listening in the kitchen when Jessica had called Miranda to set the whole thing up. At least she didn't have to lie around imagining Jessica in Ryan's arms all night. Not *this* night anyway.

The speedboat buzzed by again, closer to the beach. The engine sounded much louder from that shortened distance. "That idiot's going to hit a buoy in the dark," Elizabeth predicted to the empty room. Thankfully there weren't any swimmers to worry about so late at night.

Elizabeth sat up on the bed, toying with the idea of calling Ryan. Not that he'd answer the phone. *He might, though,* she thought. *He might think I was Arthur calling about Patti, and then he'd* have *to answer!* Of course, there was no way of predicting how Ryan would react once he found out the caller was Elizabeth.

I could try going over there. . . .

No. Bad idea. What if Ryan slammed the

door in her face again? What if he was drunk?

I should try Arthur Yager again. Elizabeth had called him earlier, along with the hospitals, but he hadn't answered. *He's probably with Patti somewhere,* she realized. *Unless he's come home by now—*

The whine of the speedboat cut through the silence again, this time very close. "He must be practically on the sand!" Elizabeth exclaimed. If the driver was foolish enough to come inside the buoys, the boat could easily get caught in the surf and be overturned.

Elizabeth got off her bed and walked to the window, wondering if she should call the Harbor Patrol. She was still deliberating when she heard a second sound—one that made her blood run cold. Somebody was screaming.

The high, thin sound floated through Elizabeth's open window, raising goose bumps on the back of her neck. The voice belonged to a woman, and she sounded terrified. As Elizabeth stood frozen with indecision another scream cut the night, this one louder. It sounded like panic, like desperation. It sounded like . . .

Jessica!

"That's impossible!" Elizabeth gasped, straining out against the windowsill. It was too dark to see the boat, but Elizabeth made out a flash of white water as the speedboat cut a dangerously tight turn. The driver *was* in the surf zone! He was going to get himself—and whoever else was on his boat—killed that way!

"Please don't let it be Jessica," Elizabeth prayed under her breath as another scream drifted across the dark beach. But intuition told her it *was* her sister out there on that boat, that it *was* her sister screaming, terrified. Fearing the worst, Elizabeth tore herself away from the window and raced down the stairs to the telephone.

Miranda answered on the second ring. "Hey, Elizabeth. What's up?"

"Is Jessica there?" Elizabeth asked nervously.

"No. Why? Is something wrong?"

"I thought she was staying with you tonight," Elizabeth insisted.

"No." Miranda sounded baffled. "Jessica had a date with Ryan. Didn't she tell you?"

I should have known! Elizabeth thought angrily. *That call to Miranda was a big fake for my benefit!*

But as quickly as Elizabeth's anger had flared, it passed, a cold dread taking its place instead. Jessica was on that boat—Elizabeth was sure of it now. Jessica and Ryan. Ryan still had access to the boat keys; he knew how to drive the rescue boats. Judging from the way he was driving, though, *Ryan* was the one who was going to need rescuing. He had to be drunk out of his mind to be risking two lives that way.

"Get Theo and drive to the marina," Elizabeth told Miranda. "Hurry!"

"What's—"

"Just go!" Elizabeth interrupted. "I'll meet you there." Miranda was still sputtering as Elizabeth slammed down the phone.

"Ben!" Elizabeth shouted. "Ben, come here!"

A second later the door to Ben's bedroom burst open and Ben and Priya came tumbling out. Ben was dressed in jeans and a flannel shirt, but Priya was still wearing her lifeguard suit and jacket, along with a pair of Ben's University of Chicago sweatpants.

"What is it?" Ben demanded, clearly alarmed by Elizabeth's tone. "What's the matter?"

"There's trouble on the water—come on!" Elizabeth cried. She sprinted out the front door, Ben and Priya hard on her heels.

Chapter
Eleven

"Ryan! Stop this boat *now!*" Jessica demanded, desperate to regain control of an out-of-control situation. They were temporarily back on the safe side of the buoys, but Ryan was still driving like a maniac.

"*Please* stop," she added imploringly. "You're going to kill us both."

"How do you know that isn't the plan?" Ryan asked, laughing harshly. "Maybe that's exactly what I have in mind." He spun the wheel to the left, then the right, then the left again, steering the boat in erratic zigzags.

"Ryan, please! You're scaring me!"

Ryan smiled and gave the boat more throttle.

Jessica grabbed for a handrail on the center steering console, fighting desperately to stay on her feet as Ryan slammed the boat through a few more turns. The speedboat bucked and whined beneath them, buffeted by the swells and currents, and Jessica had to fight back tears. She was so afraid, so helpless. She didn't even recognize this crazy guy behind the steering wheel.

If only I knew what to say to him—something to make him come to his senses, Jessica thought, holding on for dear life. But with Ryan weaving through the waves the way he was, she couldn't concentrate. Besides, she'd already tried everything: demanding, reasoning, screaming, pleading—none of it had worked. She was at her wits' end.

Suddenly Ryan spun the boat through a complete 360-degree turn. Jessica closed her eyes and gripped the rail harder, terrified. But when she opened them again, she saw the most welcome sight of her entire life. Another boat was racing across the water to their right, and it was heading straight for them!

It's a rescue boat! she thought with relief. *Someone must have reported us to the Harbor Patrol!* Ryan would go to jail now or get a ticket or *something.* In any event, Jessica had a new ride back to dry land. She pulled herself up straighter, her entire body shaking with relief. "You'd better knock it off, Ryan," she said smugly. "Or *you're* going to be in a lot of trouble."

Ryan turned his head to see what she was talking about. Then, instead of slowing down and driving normally, he steered directly at the bow of the oncoming craft. The two boats sped through the water on a collision course, the distance between them closing by the second.

"Ryan! Stop it!" Jessica screamed, her temporary smugness vanishing.

"Don't worry," he said calmly. "They'll turn."

"What if they don't?"

"They will."

Jessica could see the red and green running lights of the other boat clearly now and could make out the shape of its hull in the darkness. Desperate to warn it away, Jessica grabbed the emergency flashlight and switched it on, aiming it at the other vessel. She gasped as the second boat was caught in the beam of light and its occupants were revealed.

The driver was Elizabeth, accompanied by Ben and Priya! Stunned, Jessica tried to understand why—understand *how*—her three current sworn enemies were coming to her rescue, but a second later she knew there was no time for questions.

"Liz! Turn off!" she screamed. "He's crazy!"

The boats were practically on top of each other when Elizabeth spun her wheel and veered away. Ryan maintained his course, however, speeding directly through the patch of water Elizabeth's boat had occupied only a split second before.

"What are you doing? You could have killed her!" Jessica screamed at him, but Ryan didn't respond. Instead he swayed slightly at the wheel, as if suddenly seasick. *He's still plastered,* Jessica realized with awe. *He hasn't sobered up a bit!*

Meanwhile Elizabeth's boat had swung around in a broad turn and was pulling up alongside them.

"Ryan!" Ben shouted, his hands cupped around his mouth like a megaphone. "What are you doing? Slow down!"

That seemed to snap Ryan out of his stupor. "I hate that conceited waste of space," he muttered, his glassy eyes narrowing. "College boy! He thinks he's so much smarter than everybody else."

"Ryan! Stop the boat!" Ben urged.

A twisted smile crossed Ryan's lips. "Come and get me, college boy!"

Giving the boat full throttle, Ryan turned off toward the beach, speeding back into the surf zone. He blew past the buoys and steered his craft right up to the edge of the breaking waves. The boat rose and rocked with each passing swell, and Jessica felt sick with fear. If Ryan wasn't careful, they were going to accidentally catch a wave and capsize!

Jessica looked longingly back over her shoulder, wishing she were safe in Elizabeth's boat. But to her astonishment, Elizabeth was following them into the danger zone! "No, Liz! Go back!" Jessica yelled, tears of love and remorse springing to her eyes. It seemed impossible that after everything that had happened between them, Elizabeth was still willing to risk her life to save her twin's.

Tearing her gaze from the boat behind her, Jessica looked forward again just in time to see the steep slope of a building wave dropping away before them. They were in the surf, right on the verge of being caught. The nose of the boat tilted down abruptly.

"Ryan!" Jessica screamed. But it was too late. The boat started sliding smoothly down the face of the wave and then was lifted suddenly from behind as the wave began to crest. The stern of the boat pitched up and forward while the bow buried itself point-down in the water. They were going over!

Jessica tried to scream, to grab a railing, but everything was happening too quickly. The wave kept coming, flipping the stern up and over the bow. Jessica experienced a single agonizing second of weightlessness. Then she splashed into the cold black water, the giant wave crashing down over her head.

"David! Oh, David, why were you taken away from me?"

Nina heard the sound as if in a dream, the loud, keening cry cutting through the blackness in her brain. She gasped for air, trying to clear the cobwebs.

"Nina! Nina, are you all right?" another voice asked—a man's voice, frantic with concern.

Stu! Nina thought, her lips curling into a smile. *He's OK!* Her eyes fluttered open to meet the wet, crystal blue ones gazing worriedly down at her. "You made it," she croaked, her throat sore where Rachel had tried to choke her.

"Me!" he responded with disbelief. "What about you? I thought you were dead!"

Nina tried to lift her head, then groaned as a wave of nausea swept over her. "That was probably the plan. Help me up, will you?"

"David . . . David . . . David . . . David . . . David." Rachel's wailing had settled into an eerie, pointless chant. As Stu helped Nina carefully into a sitting position, his protective arms still around her, Nina got her first good look at the other girl, crouched on the floor a few feet away. The sight made her gasp in shock.

Rachel's short platinum hair hung in wet strands over her eyes, which streamed with tears and ruined mascara. She rocked back and forth rhythmically as she called out the name, almost as if she hoped to conjure David up out of nothing. When her eyes met Nina's, she stopped her rocking abruptly. "Do you know where David went?" she asked, her tone conversational.

"No," Nina replied. Disentangling herself from Stu, she moved closer to the other girl. "Why don't you tell me?" she prompted gently, her tone kind and understanding.

"Oh, he can't have gone very far," Rachel said. "He'll probably be back in a minute."

Nina glanced uncomprehendingly at Stu.

Then slowly, with extreme caution, Nina turned her attention back to Rachel. "I don't know who David is, Rachel," she said. "But I don't think he's coming back."

"Of course he's coming back!" Rachel snapped, her eyes flashing momentarily before the fire drained back out of them. "I just don't know when. It's been so long."

"Who's David?" Stu asked.

"Who's *David?*" Rachel repeated. Her tone was amused, as if everyone knew David. "*Only* my best friend. My very best friend in the entire world. We're going to get married when we grow up."

"When you grow up?" Nina echoed, confused.

"Yeah. My mom won't even let us go steady yet, but next year, when we're in sixth grade, she'll have to let me. Then David is going to buy me a promise ring and all you horrible girls will be jealous. I can't wait!"

"Rachel," Nina said softly, trying to understand what was happening. "You know this isn't sixth grade, right?"

"Duh!" Rachel responded sarcastically. "It's only fifth. But sixth will be here soon, and then you'll see. All you stupid girls who make fun of me—who tease me because I stutter—you're all going to wish you were me next year!"

"I never teased you for stuttering," Nina protested. "You don't even *have* a stutter."

Rachel glared at her suspiciously. "You're

lying. But David doesn't mind it. He's *nice*—not like the rest of you kids."

"So where's David now?" Stu cut in. "He isn't here."

Rachel opened her mouth to answer, then suddenly started rocking again. "I don't know," she said, her voice strained and older sounding. "You said he was coming right back."

"No," Nina corrected gently. "*You* said he was coming right back. Where did he go?"

"Nowhere! I mean, just across the street. He's going to buy us some candy bars at the liquor store."

"He went to the *liquor* store?" Nina repeated, baffled.

"No, just across the street. He's in the street." Rachel's almond-shaped eyes went suddenly huge, and her head snapped back in horror. "David!" she screamed. "David, no! Watch out!"

"Rachel—," Nina began, cringing.

"Noooo!" Rachel screamed. "Oh, please, no!" Her eyes were wide and unfocused, fixed on something only she could see. "David! David!" She threw herself down on the floor, writhing in pain.

Nina and Stu watched, horrified, as Rachel squirmed over to the meditation pillow and took it into her arms, lifting it up slightly off the floor. "No . . . no . . . no," she mumbled. She lowered her head tenderly, pressing one cheek to the pillow. "No . . . no . . . please. Not David."

Nina's heart filled with sudden, unexpected pity. "Rachel, it's only a pillow," she said slowly, reaching over to place a comforting arm around the other girl's heaving shoulders. "That's not David."

Rachel looked up, and her eyes locked with Nina's. "Of course not," she agreed sadly, strangely lucid. "David's dead."

"Dead!" Nina gasped.

"Didn't you see him get run down by that car?" Rachel dropped her head back to the pillow, sobbing softly. "Right in front of me," she moaned through her tears. "He got killed right in front of me."

Without thinking, Nina drew Rachel into her arms and hugged her tightly, sympathy overwhelming her. No wonder she'd turned out the way she had! Rachel dropped the meditation pillow and cried with abandon, her head on Nina's shoulder. Stu looked on helplessly, his eyes asking Nina what to do.

"Go call someone, Stu," Nina directed softly. "Get some help."

Stu nodded gratefully and quickly left the room.

"He'll call the police," Rachel said from Nina's shoulder, her voice oddly flat and detached.

"Uh . . . probably," Nina admitted. "But we won't let them do anything bad to you. We'll tell them what's happened and make sure you get some help, that's all."

"Help!" Rachel scoffed in that same flat

voice. "All the shrinks in the world can't bring back my David."

"No," Nina murmured sadly. But then another thought occurred to her. "Rachel . . . why did you lie about being pregnant?"

Rachel lifted her head long enough to shoot Nina a wounded glance before she dropped it again, defeated. "I didn't lie. David always told me that if I wished hard enough, anything could come true." With that the tears began once more. "All I wanted was someone to love me again," Rachel sobbed. "Someone who'd know the real me, just like David."

"I'm sorry, Rachel," Nina told her, biting back tears of her own as she stroked the crying girl's back. "I'm really, really sorry."

Help! Help! Jessica screamed mentally as the freezing water closed in from all sides. *Somebody help me!* She struggled desperately in the churning current, wondering wildly how deep the water was, how close to the beach she was, where the capsized rescue boat might be. *I'm going to die,* whimpered a terrified voice at the back of her brain.

No! No, you're not. Shut up! she answered back fiercely. *Keep swimming!*

But Jessica had barely had time to catch a breath before she'd been pushed underwater, and now her lungs burned from the lack of oxygen. She frog-kicked erratically, completely disoriented. *Which way is the surface?* she wondered desperately. In the total darkness of the nighttime sea Jessica had no idea. And she had to breathe. She *had* to. . . .

What if I'm swimming the wrong way? The thought made her weak with panic. *What if I'm swimming down instead of up?* The idea was so frightening that Jessica stopped kicking momentarily, paralyzed with fear. *I've got to breathe. I've got to breathe! Just pick a direction and swim!* But her body wouldn't obey her. Only then did Jessica realize she was still moving, even though she'd stopped kicking. Her motionless form was being carried through the water column, naturally floating upward.

That's the way! she told herself excitedly, beginning to swim with all her strength. Seconds later she broke the surface and wheezed for air.

"Help! *Help!*" she sputtered into the night. She treaded water in a circle as she scanned the area around her. If she'd come up near the overturned boat, she was still in terrible danger. The next wave could smash the boat into her, breaking bones or, worse, knocking her unconscious.

"*Jessica!* Where are you?" Elizabeth's voice sounded frantic and faraway.

"Liz! Help!" Jessica screamed before another cresting wave covered her head.

Don't fight it, Jessica advised herself, trying not to panic. *Wait to float up again.* The strength of the confused currents gradually diminished, and Jessica felt herself moving in the direction of the surface. Kicking swiftly, she broke back into the air. "Help!"

"Hang on, Jess!" yelled a high-pitched female voice—Priya's. "We're coming!"

"Help!" Ryan cried out suddenly from the opposite direction. "Over here!"

"No way! Over here!" Jessica screeched. Ryan could drown for all she cared. "Help *me!*"

She had begun swimming in the direction of Priya's voice when all of a sudden she saw something big in the water to her left, something just barely breaking the surface.

It was the overturned boat.

Jessica shivered with both cold and fear as she stroked quickly past the boat, trying to get far away from it before the next wave came.

"Jessica! Where are you?" Elizabeth's voice drifted through the night. "We can't bring the boat into the surf. You have to swim to us!"

"I'm trying!" Jessica yelled, but Elizabeth's voice sounded as if it were getting farther away rather than closer. Another wave began building to Jessica's left, and she dove to avoid getting clobbered. As her head resurfaced, though, she suddenly realized she'd been swimming in the wrong direction. The rescue boat had to stay outside the surf line. If Jessica wanted to reach it, she'd have to swim out to sea— *into* the waves, not parallel to them.

She adjusted her direction and began swimming again. Her arms felt like lead, and her feet were numb and heavy as they flutter-kicked in the cold water. *Just keep going,* Jessica encouraged herself. *It can't be that much farther.* But she was so cold and, suddenly, so tired. She could barely lift her arms to stroke.

"Help! Over here!" Ryan called again. His voice was much closer than before.

"Yes! Over here!" Jessica echoed. She could swim that far, if only the boat would come in as far as Ryan.

"We can't come in there!" Priya shouted. "Swim!"

"I can't!" Jessica screamed, tears of fear and frustration mixing with the salt water on her face. "Liz, I can't!" She was so cold . . . so tired. . . .

"Swim, Jessica!" Ben shouted.

"No!" Another wave came in, and Jessica went under. She held her breath, not even struggling, as the ocean tossed her about like an old rag doll. She was beyond fear now, beyond hope too. Whatever was going to happen would happen. She could only wait.

When at last her head popped through the surface, Jessica's eyes were dazzled by a sudden beam of light. Someone was shining a powerful flashlight in her direction!

"There she is!" she heard Ben shout. "Go, go, go! Now!"

An engine roared and Elizabeth's boat streaked across the water toward her, risking a daring rescue in the short interval between waves. Jessica's throat felt thick with gratitude as she waved her hands over her head to signal the boat. They had to hurry—the boat had to get in and get out fast—or they'd *all* end up dead.

"Liz!" Jessica yelled. "Over here!"

"Elizabeth!" Ryan shouted from a short distance away. "Help me!"

The flashlight beam swung away from Jessica, picking up Ryan's bobbing head instead.

"I've got them both! Drive in between them," Ben yelled.

The boat pulled up within thirty feet, and Elizabeth threw the throttle into reverse to stop its progress into the surf. With a burst of renewed strength Jessica put down her head and started swimming for all she was worth. Moments later her fingers brushed the smooth fiberglass surface of the hull and she looked up into Priya's impassive face.

"Take my hand," Priya said coolly, standing ready to hoist Jessica into the boat.

Jessica hesitated. The last thing she wanted was to touch Priya Rahman. Just because the stuck-up little princess had somehow been coerced into helping didn't mean Jessica wanted anything to do with her. Why couldn't Elizabeth help her into the boat? Or even Ben?

"Come on, Jessica! Let's go!" Priya urged.

The ice in her eyes had melted slightly, but Jessica returned her enemy's gaze with loathing, unwilling to give her one more thing to lord over her.

From the other side of the boat Jessica heard her sister's voice. "Grab him, Ben! Help me out here."

The two of them must be rescuing Ryan, Jessica realized. It suddenly looked as if her choices were Priya or nothing, but Jessica still couldn't bring herself to take the other girl's hand.

I can't give in, she thought. *Not to* her. *I'd be better off trying to climb into the boat myself.* But even as she thought it, Jessica knew it was impossible. There was no way she was going to be able to pull herself out of the water and over the high, slippery side of the rescue boat on her own.

I'll wait, Jessica decided. *Ben and Elizabeth will finish helping Ryan and then they'll come over for me.*

Just then, however, Jessica became aware of the current sucking back out to sea. Another wave was building. If the rescue boat didn't get turned around and back out past the swells, it was going to be flipped over in the surf exactly as Ryan's boat had been.

"Jessica! Come on, just take my hand!" Priya screamed hysterically. "I'm sorry, all right? Everything I said—I take it all back! Just hurry! *Please!*"

Chapter Twelve

"Please tell me, Guru Futi," Wendy repeated eagerly, squeezing his hands. "What did Pedro tell you? What does he say about our marriage?"

The guru's eyes seemed to refocus gradually. He lowered his gaze, then started slightly, as if just suddenly seeing Wendy in front of him. "Get up, my child," he said gently. "You mustn't kneel to me."

Winston heaved an enormous sigh of relief and sank back onto the cream-colored carpeting. *What an actor!* he thought proudly. *I must be a killer coach!*

When Pedro had done that fake fit thing, with the trembling and all, Winston had been convinced that they were going to need an ambulance. And he *knew* the guru was a fake! Completely satisfied that his plan was going off without a hitch, Winston leaned back against the silk-covered wall and settled in to watch the scene playing out in front of him.

Pedro had convinced Wendy to sit in her chair again, but she still held his hands clasped tightly in hers, straining forward across the small distance between their seats.

"Pedro loves you more than anything else," the "guru" intoned solemnly. "More than anyone he knows, more than touring. More than music, even."

"But how can that be true?" Wendy asked, her clear gray eyes searching Pedro's brown ones. "I never even see him anymore. If he loves me so much, why is he never around?"

Pedro paused a moment, as if to get more information. "Pedro says he had a career before he met you. He thought you understood that. Being away from you isn't easy for him either, but he's trying to build something for the future. For himself, for you . . . and for the children he hopes you'll have together someday."

"Children?" Wendy whispered, her eyes filling with tears. "He wants a family?"

"He's told you that before."

"Well, he's mentioned it," Wendy admitted. "But how could I believe him when he was always getting on a plane the next day? I need someone who's there for me all the time. Like Winston." Tears ran freely down her face. Wendy made no attempt to dry them.

"You think that because Pedro has to work, it means he doesn't love you?"

"No, but—"

"But you've decided that you love Winston instead?"

"Yes. No. I don't know. Oh, Guru Futi, it's like I'm dying inside," Wendy said, her voice catching. "I miss him. You have no idea how much I miss him."

Pedro pulled Wendy's clasped hands closer and leaned forward. "If Pedro were here right now, what would you tell him?"

Wendy paused a moment, then rushed recklessly ahead, the words pouring out of her. "That I love him. So much. Please don't leave me, Pedro. I don't want us to be apart. I . . . I don't love Winston. I love you." She sobbed as she spoke, her heart clearly breaking.

Tears welled up in Pedro's eyes to match the ones streaming from Wendy's. "Pedro has heard you, Wendy. He knows how you feel. He's happier than he's ever been before in his life."

"Do you think so?" Wendy asked hopefully. "Do you think he still loves me?"

"I *know* he still loves you. More every day."

Wendy smiled a little in spite of her tears. "I wish I could be sure about that."

Pedro smiled back, and the corners of his mouth twitched slightly beneath the gray mustache. "You doubt my powers?"

"No!" Wendy said hurriedly. "Not at all. It's just that . . . well . . . it would be nice to hear it directly from Pedro."

"I see." He sat back in his chair. "Then perhaps this will help." He closed his eyes, drew in his breath, and began singing softly.

> The girl with smoke-colored eyes
> Has set my soul on fire. . . .

Pedro's voice shook slightly as he sang the ballad he'd written for Wendy the previous summer, when they'd very first fallen in love. Wendy's face registered her surprise, but she sat listening intently, trying to understand what was happening, as Pedro kept on singing.

> She came up from the waters
> She came down from the skies. . . .

Pedro's voice had steadied; the words rang strong and true in the spacious hotel suite. His eyes remained closed as he felt his way around the music, putting everything he had into the tender love song. He gently caressed each note, every nuance.

> Her laughter sounds like summer
> I cannot live without her—

"Pedro!" Wendy cried suddenly, jumping out of her chair. "Oh, Pedro! Is it you?"

Pedro stopped singing and stood up, removing his wig and mustache with a sheepish grin.

"I . . . I . . . what are you *doing* here?" Wendy demanded.

The singer looked embarrassed. "I'm sorry, Wendy. I didn't want to fool you. It's just that I love you so much—"

But before he could finish his sentence, Wendy threw herself into his arms, weeping uncontrollable tears of joy. "Pedro! I can't believe you came back for me!"

"Are you kidding? I'd do anything for you, Wendy. Anything." Pedro's cheeks were glistening too, and Winston suspected his friend's tears were as much from relief as happiness. Pedro kissed his wife tenderly, lovingly.

"Oh, Pedro," Wendy whispered huskily.

Winston suddenly realized that the two of them had forgotten he was in the room. He cleared his throat self-consciously. "I, uh, I guess I'll find my own way out," he said, rising and backing toward the door.

Neither Wendy nor Pedro showed any sign of being aware of his presence. They clung to each other, passionately returning each other's kisses.

"OK! I'm *leaving* now!" Winston opened the hotel suite door, and the sudden crosscurrent of air caused the silk on the walls to rustle.

The candles flickered as incense drifted lazily through the room. Wendy and Pedro held each other tightly, the gentle reverberation of the distantly crashing surf the only sound; the gauzy curtains on either side of the open French doors fluttered out into the starry night.

"Wow," Winston breathed, momentarily frozen by the scene before him. It was all so beautiful and . . . well . . . *romantic*. He could feel himself choking up as he slipped out through the doorway, closing the door silently behind him.

Now, don't you go getting all teary eyed too, Egbert, he reprimanded himself as he walked back out to the parking lot. But it was too late. Thinking about the happy couple he'd just reunited made Winston feel mushy all over.

"*Please,* Jess!" Priya screamed again, her hand straining toward the water.

Jessica could sense the swell building behind the boat. They had only seconds to get out of there before the wave came crashing down on top of them. Still, there were worse things in life than drowning. Putting up with Priya, for instance.

"You swear you're really sorry?" Jessica asked.

"Yes! I swear!"

Hesitating only a second longer, Jessica grabbed Priya's hand. The other girl immediately hoisted her into the boat with the superhuman strength born of fear. Jessica slid down into the bottom of the boat just as Ryan was lifted in from the other side.

"That's it! Let's go!" Ben cried.

Elizabeth sprang to the steering console and threw the boat into gear, spinning the wheel hard to turn the boat into the oncoming surf. The wave was building rapidly, becoming a towering wall of water in front of the little vessel.

"We're not going to make it," Ben yelled as Elizabeth gave the boat full throttle.

The rescue boat leaped forward and headed straight at the approaching wave. "Oh, wow. Oh, wow. Oh, wow," Priya chanted nervously. "Oh, wow. Here we go."

The boat reached the base of the wave and tilted up abruptly as it began climbing the face. Priya and Ben staggered backward, then managed to grab rails on the console to keep from falling. Elizabeth held on to the steering wheel desperately, her face white with fear and her eyes fixed forward on the crest of the wave. Jessica remained huddled in the bottom of the boat near Ryan, her hands laced tightly around the only thing she could grab—Priya's ankle.

"Faster, Liz!" Ben shouted, pushing at the throttle. But the lever was already forward as far as it would go.

"That's it! That's all!" Elizabeth yelled in return.

The boat kept rising, rising. All the loose

items in the hull slid, then tumbled madly toward the stern. It felt as if they were going almost straight up. In front of them the crest of the wave curled over, seeming to hesitate over the bow.

"Hang on!" Elizabeth screamed.

Water crashed down on them, filling the boat. Jessica screamed, her fingernails digging deep into the flesh of Priya's ankle. Then, just as suddenly, the boat shot through the wave on the other side and they were falling. The boat fishtailed wildly down the back of the breaking wave, still pointed out to sea.

"We made it!" Ben shouted triumphantly, slapping Elizabeth on the back. "Way to drive!"

Elizabeth nodded but didn't break her concentration until she'd taken the boat all the way out through the surf zone and back into safe, open water. Then she threw the boat into neutral and crouched at her sister's side. "Are you OK, Jess?" she asked, her expression strained.

"Yeah. Thanks to you," Jessica replied. "I owe you."

Elizabeth shook her head. "Not me. But maybe Ben and Priya."

"Not me," Ben said quickly. "Just doing our jobs, right, Priya?"

Priya hesitated, then glanced down at Jessica. "You're welcome," she said. But her voice sounded marginally less haughty than usual. "I . . . I'm glad I could help."

Stunned, Jessica searched the other girl's face for signs of sarcasm. To her amazement, Priya seemed sincere. Far from dripping with the expected venom, Priya's dark eyes seemed shaken but relieved.

After the way she just risked her neck for me, I guess I ought to make some sort of effort to patch things up, Jessica thought grudgingly. She pulled herself to her feet and forced a small smile to her lips. "Truce?" she asked, extending her right hand warily toward Priya.

Priya glanced nervously at Ben, then took Jessica's hand and shook it briefly. "Truce."

"I'm sorry about your ankle," Jessica told her, almost meaning it. "I was really scared, and there was nothing else to hold on to."

Priya looked down at the ugly gashes Jessica's manicured fingernails had left behind. "Me too," she admitted. "I didn't even feel that."

The group stood there awkwardly a moment before Elizabeth glanced over at the other side of the boat. "Ryan, are you hurt?" she asked suddenly. Ryan was still lying on his side in the bottom, making no move to stand up.

"No," he returned in a dazed, shell-shocked voice.

"Do you want some help up?"

"No."

"Come on, buddy," Ben urged, leaning down to help him anyway. "You'll be more comfortable on the trip back home if you at least sit up." At Ben's insistence Ryan finally propped himself into a sitting position against one corner of the stern.

Jessica looked at him then, expecting to feel nothing but loathing, but the sight of Ryan's frozen, stricken expression took her by surprise, turning her revulsion into something more like pity. Not sympathy, and definitely not forgiveness, but perhaps the first inklings of true understanding. Elizabeth was right—Ryan *did* have a problem. A terrible, insidious problem that had almost cost her her life.

A trickle of blood ran down Ryan's cheek from a cut above his eyebrow. Jessica shuddered as she watched it trace a path to his chin.

"Do you even know what you just did?" she asked him quietly, her voice shaking slightly. "You could have killed every single person on this boat."

Ryan turned to meet her gaze, his eyes zombie blank.

"You almost killed us!" she repeated, more loudly.

Ryan shrugged slightly. "Sorry." His voice was hollow, detached. Not there.

Jessica whirled away from him, the last remnants of her so-called romance crashing down around her. A second later she was vomiting salt water over the railing.

*　　　*　　　*

The final police car disappeared into darkness, swallowed up in the totally lightless night sky around SeaMist Island. Nina was surprised at how depressed she felt as she watched it carry Rachel Max away.

"I can't believe I'm saying this." She sighed, snuggling in tight against Stu's comforting shoulder. "But I actually feel awful about turning Rachel over to the police."

Stu nodded, his expression pained. "I know. Believe me, I feel totally responsible. I never should have gotten mixed up with someone so disturbed in the first place."

"You didn't know," Nina soothed, guiding him back toward the house. "None of us did."

"Still . . . what do you think will happen to her?"

"The officer said that if we didn't press charges, she'd either be released or committed to County Mental Health for a while," Nina reminded him. "Since we're not pressing charges, hopefully she'll go to County."

They reached the front door and walked into Stu's enormously expensive home. Stu glanced around the entryway distractedly, clearly upset. "I can't bear to think of her at some freaky government loony bin—it'll probably just make her worse. Meditation would help her the most, I'll bet. If she could locate her center, the rest would follow."

"Well, I doubt they do a lot of meditating

194

where Rachel's going, but I don't know what we can do about it," Nina said. "I feel bad too, but we couldn't just put her back on the street. She's nuts!"

Stu sighed. "I know." Then all of a sudden his face lit up. "Listen, Nina, why can't I pay for Rachel to go somewhere nice? Someplace where they'll really give her the help she needs? I can afford it. Why not use all this money to do some good for a change?"

Nina stared in disbelief. "Let me get this straight. This woman stalked you, lied to you about having your baby, and attacked me in your home, and now you want to foot the bill to send her to a fancy private sanitarium?"

Stu's face fell. "You think it's a bad idea."

Nina reached for him, her arms twining around his neck and drawing his face down toward hers. "Quite the contrary," she said softly. "I think it's the most incredibly selfless thing I've ever heard. Do you even breathe the same air as the rest of us?"

"It's nothing," Stu protested, blushing. "It's only money."

"It's more than money, Stu," Nina insisted. "I'm completely blown away by how you're always thinking of everyone else, always doing the sweetest things. . . ."

"Stop it," Stu begged. "You're embarrassing me."

"When I washed up on your beach, I went

out of my way to be the biggest pain in the neck that anyone ever met. But no matter what I did, it didn't faze you in the slightest. You just kept right on being nice to me."

Stu smiled at the memory. "I could tell you were really a good person. Deep down, I mean."

Nina laughed. "Not that deep, I hope. But that's what I'm talking about, Stu. You always believe the best of everyone."

Stu shrugged off her compliments, obviously still embarrassed. "Well, if you're feeling guilty about the way you treated me the day we met, I'll be happy to let you make it up to me now."

"Oh yeah?" Nina said, her smile crinkling the corners of her eyes. "What did you have in mind?"

"I don't know. Maybe a full shiatsu massage. Do you know how to do shiatsu?"

"No, but I know how to do this," Nina replied, bringing her mouth to his. She melted up against him, kissing him with everything she had. It felt incredible to have her arms around him now, knowing there was nothing standing in the way of their happiness. The passionate kiss continued until Stu's lips curved into a happy grin against her own.

"This is better anyway," he murmured.

"I love you, Stu Kirkwood," she whispered before she even knew she was going to.

"I love you too."

*   *   *

"Are you sure you're going to be OK?" Elizabeth asked her twin anxiously.

Jessica had seemed all right when they'd first picked her up, but after the confrontation with Ryan she'd become silent and withdrawn, shivering convulsively. Jessica nodded slowly, staring off into space.

They were standing on the main dock, where Jessica's sodden black minidress provided no protection against the cool breeze off the ocean. Miranda and Theo had been waiting on the dock when the rescue boat came in, but Miranda had taken one quick look at Jessica and immediately run off to fetch a blanket. In the meantime, though, Jessica was clearly freezing. Her bare arms and legs were a mass of goose bumps. "I can't believe I almost died for that guy," she said dully.

Elizabeth felt a sudden, fierce blaze of anger. How could Ryan have been so stupid as to endanger Jessica's life in addition to his own? It would have been awful enough if Ryan had been killed, but Elizabeth couldn't even imagine life without Jessica. If her sister had drowned, Elizabeth would never, *never* have been able to forgive Ryan.

Ryan's an alcoholic. He can't control himself when he's drinking, Elizabeth reminded herself, but it didn't help. Standing there looking at her devastated sister, she could only conclude that

Ryan had better *find* a way to control himself—and fast—if he wanted anyone to have anything more to do with him.

"I'm sorry about all this, Jess," she said. "I tried to warn you, but . . . I know it's hard."

Jessica looked vaguely annoyed.

"I'm not saying I told you so!" Elizabeth hurried to clarify. She hugged her twin close in spite of her soaking wet clothing. "Do you have any idea how happy I am that you weren't hurt? When I think about what could have happened—" Elizabeth broke off with a shudder.

"I don't want to talk about it," Jessica murmured.

Just then Miranda came running up with the blanket and threw it around Jessica's shoulders. "Are you OK, Jess?" she asked worriedly.

"I think she's in shock," Elizabeth answered for her twin, rubbing Jessica's shoulders through the rough warm wool of the blanket. "We need to get her inside."

"The Harbor Master's office is open, and I turned on the heater in the lobby," Miranda replied. "Come on, Jessica. Let's go warm you up."

"I'll be there in a minute, Jess," Elizabeth called as Miranda began leading Jessica off the dock. "I'm just going to check on Ryan first."

"Don't worry about us," Miranda reassured her. "I'll take care of Jessica, and Theo will drive us home as soon as he's done here."

"Thanks, Miranda," Elizabeth said gratefully. "I'd rather go with you guys, but somebody needs to make sure that Ryan gets home all right."

"No problem," Miranda said, waving off Elizabeth's thanks.

Elizabeth watched the two girls walking away down the dock—Jessica's huddled, shivering form tucked in against Miranda's tall, athletic frame. It would be so much nicer to fuss over Jessica with blankets and hot chocolate than to deal with Ryan. Elizabeth's heart pounded furiously at the thought of even speaking to him. She was still so angry, there was no telling what she'd say.

Drawing a deep breath, Elizabeth squared her shoulders and walked back to the rescue boat, where Theo was busy applying first aid to the cut over Ryan's eyebrow. Ben and Priya had gone with the Harbor Patrol to try to recover the capsized boat, leaving only Elizabeth, Ryan, and Theo behind on the creaking dock.

"Sorry, Ryan," Theo apologized as he dabbed iodine on Ryan's open wound. "I know that has to hurt."

Ryan shrugged. "Not enough."

Not as much as he deserves, he means, Elizabeth thought, feeling like she could read his mind. *He knows he's been a total jerk, and now he's embarrassed.*

In the year that she'd known Ryan, Elizabeth had thought she'd experienced every emotion it was remotely possible to associate with the guy. But she'd been wrong. She'd never pitied Ryan before—not until that moment.

"How are you doing?" she asked him, stepping into the boat and kneeling at his side.

Ryan averted his eyes. "OK."

"He's a little banged up, but he'll be fine," Theo offered, putting the final touches on a professional-looking dressing.

"I *am* fine," Ryan growled, standing up. His knees buckled and he lurched forward unsteadily, as if he were going to fall. Elizabeth rushed forward and grabbed him, but his arms went tight and rigid beneath her well-meaning fingers.

"I can walk by myself," he muttered, not looking at her.

"I don't think you can," she answered softly. "Please, Ryan. Let me help you."

He began to shake his head no, then gave up, relaxing into her grip.

"Thanks for everything, Theo," Elizabeth told her fellow lifeguard. "I think I can take it from here."

"Sure. No problem," Theo returned affably. He closed up his first-aid kit and stepped out onto the dock. "See you tomorrow," he added before he walked off toward the Harbor Master's office.

"Tomorrow," Elizabeth called after him. Then she turned to Ryan. "For now, though, let's concentrate on getting you home. Do you think you can walk that far?"

"Of course," he said coolly.

Elizabeth helped him climb out of the boat, and they started down the dock in silence, Ryan stiff and aloof. *I hope he's not going to act like this the entire way,* Elizabeth couldn't help thinking, sneaking a glance at his closed, sullen profile. *If only he would open up and tell me what he's feeling. Tell me what's happened to Patti!*

But for the first time ever, Elizabeth had to accept the fact that changing Ryan was a lost cause. She'd be happy if she just got him home without hurting anyone else.

_____

Chapter Thirteen

"Here. Put these on," Elizabeth said, handing Ryan a pair of dry sweatpants. "You're soaked!" she added defensively when she saw the poisonous look he shot her.

"Fine." Ryan grabbed the sweatpants and stepped into the bathroom, closing the door loudly.

Elizabeth was left behind in his dingy, messy room. There were dirty towels strewn everywhere, rumpled clothing, half-empty whiskey glasses. Ryan would never have allowed such a mess when he was sober, let alone have *made* it. It was just another sign of how far he'd fallen. Crossing to the sofa, Elizabeth picked up the discarded clothing there and tossed it onto the floor, finding a lightly worn sweatshirt in the process.

Ryan opened the bathroom door. "I'm dry. Are you satisfied?" he grumbled.

"Here. I found a clean sweatshirt too," Elizabeth

said, holding it out. She tried to force her voice to sound cheerful, but Ryan didn't seem fooled.

He took the shirt and pulled it over his head, then sank down on the couch. "It's late," he said without looking at her. "You should get going."

"I know. I will." Elizabeth hesitated, then took a deep breath and rushed ahead. "But Ryan, you've got to tell me . . . what happened to Patti? Please. I . . . I need to know."

Ryan's head snapped up as if she'd slapped him. His eyes flashed dangerously, but still he didn't answer.

"Is she . . . is she dead?" Elizabeth asked hesitantly.

"Of course not!" he exploded, banging his fist down on the coffee table. "What gave you a stupid idea like that?"

The unexpected violence of his outburst made Elizabeth jump. She crossed her arms over her chest and glared at him from across the room. "I'm sorry, Ryan. It's just . . . the way you were acting. And Arthur sounded so upset on the phone today."

"She had a car accident, that's all," Ryan said, massaging his temples, his voice back to normal. "She had a car accident, but she isn't dead."

Elizabeth sighed in deep relief. "I . . . I feared the worst, I guess. Now that she's drinking again, I—"

"She didn't die, OK?" Ryan's head was still

in his hands, but a note of annoyance had crept into his tone. "Drinking doesn't make you *totally* incompetent, Elizabeth. She's in intensive care, that's all."

Elizabeth's heart raced, and all the relief she'd felt only a second before evaporated instantly. "Intensive care! Ryan, that's serious! What's her condition? When did you last talk to Arthur?"

But Ryan ignored her questions. Instead of answering, he walked to his bed and sat down pointedly on its edge. "I need to sleep, Elizabeth," he said rudely. As far as he was concerned, the conversation was obviously over.

"But Ryan!" she protested. "Arthur and Patti may need you!" She glanced nervously toward his answering machine. As she'd feared, the rhythmically blinking red light showed he had a message waiting. "Don't you think you ought to at least check your messages?"

"I'll do it later," he said.

But Elizabeth was determined. "It could be Arthur," she insisted. "It could be important."

Ryan finally looked at her—*really* looked at her—and Elizabeth saw the fear in his eyes. Then he dropped his head and covered his face with his trembling hands. Elizabeth could see how hard he was struggling to keep himself together, to keep from breaking down.

She walked slowly to the answering machine and stood with one slender finger poised over the message button. "Ryan," she said gently. "Ryan, I'm pushing the button." She hesitated a moment longer, expecting him to tell her to stop, to get out of his room, to leave him alone. But Ryan sat motionless on the bed, his face still hidden in his hands.

Elizabeth pushed the button.

The answering machine jolted to life, and the strained voice of Arthur Yager cut the anxious silence.

"Hello, Ryan? It's Arthur. Listen . . . uh . . . Patti didn't make it. She's dead, Ryan. I . . . uh, I have to go. . . ."

There was the sound of a strangled sob, then silence as the message came to an end.

Elizabeth took in the horrible news in shock. *Poor Patti,* she thought sadly, wiping at her eyes. *Poor Arthur!* But first and foremost, Elizabeth's heart went out to Ryan. She knew the pain she was feeling was nothing compared to what Ryan must be going through. Patti had been his A.A. sponsor, his confidant, his friend. The two of them had helped each other succeed at the hardest thing either of them had ever done. And now Patti was gone. Just imagining the hole her loss must leave in Ryan's heart made Elizabeth feel queasy, inadequate.

She turned to him, wanting to comfort him somehow. Ryan still sat frozen on his bed, almost as if he hadn't heard.

"I'm sorry, Ryan," Elizabeth said quietly. "So sorry." She walked over to his bed and sat beside him, rubbing his back with a soothing hand.

Ryan stiffened, shuddering under her fingers.

"Don't," she whispered. "Don't be that way now. You don't want to be alone tonight."

"Elizabeth," he murmured, turning to face her. His brimming brown eyes met hers, and a second later he was pulling her into his arms, squeezing her with all his strength. "Why?"

And then came the sobs, exploding out of his body as if they'd finally found the exit.

The Saturday morning sunshine flooded the beach, making Jessica squint in spite of her dark glasses. It was going to be a beautiful day. She was glad she was around to see it.

"There you are!" Miranda called, loping across the sand to her side. Both girls were suited up, ready for Nina to hold the morning meeting and make the assignments for the day. "I can't believe you came to work this morning!" Miranda added. "It's Elizabeth's day off. Couldn't you get her to cover for you?"

Jessica shrugged. "She probably would have, if I'd asked her to. But she must be exhausted too—I fell asleep before she even came in last night. Besides, there's no reason I can't work today. I'm fine."

Miranda laughed. "You're tough, that's for

sure." She flipped at Jessica's ponytail playfully, then flexed both tan biceps in a bodybuilder's pose. "Come on, tough stuff. Let's see if you can take me."

"Very funny," Jessica returned, trying not to smile at her tall, buffed friend. "Anyway, we both know I can."

"Well, I give you an A for attitude anyway," Miranda said with a chuckle. "After what you went through last night, I can't believe you're even on the beach."

Jessica shrugged. "These things happen." Miranda raised her eyebrows, and a moment later the two friends were laughing. "I know, only to me," Jessica added, right before the sight of Priya arriving at the Main Tower turned her giggles into a groan. *Oh, great,* she thought. *Just the person I* didn't *need to see.* Priya had been half decent the night before, but Jessica wasn't naive enough to believe that such unnatural behavior would last.

A second later, though, Priya raised a tentative hand and waved, an awkward little smile on her lips. Jessica stared in amazement, unsure she'd actually just seen that.

"Did Priya Rahman *wave* at you?" Miranda wondered, clearly shocked.

"Uh, yeah," Jessica admitted, waving cautiously back. "I guess she did."

"Why?"

"Well, we kind of agreed to get off each other's case last night," Jessica replied. "I can't believe she's actually *doing* it, though."

"Wonders never cease," Miranda said sarcastically, rolling her eyes. "But if I were you, I wouldn't count on it to last."

"I'm not," Jessica assured her. "I think we both got carried away with the whole life-and-death thing. I'll be nice as long as she is, though," she added hastily. There was no way she was going to let Priya make her look bad *again!*

"Speaking of life and death," Miranda said slowly. "Have you seen Ryan yet? I mean, since . . . you know."

"No," Jessica replied, suppressing a shudder as she glanced at his front door. That was one meeting she wasn't looking forward to either. If only she'd admitted things with Ryan weren't working out! She should have dumped him hard instead of sneaking around, lying to everybody.

"Listen, Miranda," she said quickly, before she lost her nerve. "I owe you an apology. I never should have lied to you about how great things were going with Ryan and me. You've been such a good friend, and I—"

"Forget about it," Miranda interrupted, holding up one hand. "I understand. A woman in love and all that."

"But that's just the thing!" Jessica said unhappily. "I *wasn't* in love. Well, maybe I thought I was at first. But later . . . later I only wanted it to look that way to Ben and Priya—so they wouldn't think I was so pathetic." She drew in a deep, shaky breath. "I can't believe I was so stupid. Maybe those two were right about my IQ all along."

"Don't be ridiculous," Miranda scoffed. "And don't take the blame for Ryan either. You're *strong*, Jessica. Look at you—you're all suited up for a day at work when you ought to be home in bed!"

"Yeah," Jessica said slowly. "I guess. Anyway, thanks for being so great." She stepped forward and put her arms around Miranda, giving her friend an apologetic hug.

Miranda returned the hug but pulled away a second later. "Don't look now," she said under her breath, "but I think someone's coming over to talk to you."

Jessica turned with her pulse thudding hard, expecting to see Ryan. Instead Ben trudged across the sand in her direction, looking outrageously tan and handsome in the early morning light. Jessica felt her heart flip over with regret that things hadn't worked out between them, but for the first time her regret was tempered by an important realization.

Things *hadn't* worked out between them.

It was over.

The sooner she admitted it and got on with her life, the happier she'd be.

"I just wanted to see how you're feeling this morning," Ben said when he reached her side. "Are you OK?"

"Fine," Jessica returned, an embarrassed little smile on her lips. "Uh, listen, Ben. I'm sorry you had to get involved in my big adventure last night. The whole thing was pretty humiliating." She shrugged, at a loss for words. "Anyway, thanks for coming out to help me."

"What?" he said, sounding surprised. "Of *course* I helped! You . . . you'd have done the same for me. Right?"

Jessica felt a slow blush heating her cheeks. She dropped her eyes to the sand. "Sure." What she wouldn't have given to rescue Ben from a similar mess! She couldn't imagine a better way of showing him how much she still cared. Then she realized that showing he cared was exactly what *Ben* had been doing.

"Listen, Jess," he began, his voice conciliatory, his blue eyes tender. "There's been a lot of bad blood this summer, but I want you to know I still—"

"Don't say it!" she interrupted quickly. "Please, Ben. Whatever it is, it's too late."

"But I think you ought to know. I—"

"I feel the same way, all right? But it doesn't

matter anymore, does it? I mean, it doesn't change anything."

Ben looked surprised. Then, slowly, he shook his head in silent agreement. They both knew he had no intention of breaking up with Priya.

"The truth is," Jessica began, "we've been acting like fools this summer. We've all been so busy bickering that we've forgotten what we're here for."

"Which is?"

She gestured out across the sand toward the water and the first straggling groups of early morning beachgoers. "Saving lives, of course. What do you say we bury the hatchet and concentrate on being incredibly great lifeguards?"

"You really are something," Ben told her, his eyes shining with admiration. "Do you know that? After what you went through last night—"

Jessica cut him off with a shudder. "If you'd been through it, you'd feel the same way, believe me. Life's too short."

"You're right," Ben said, smiling. "Friends?" He held out his hand for Jessica to shake.

"Friends," she agreed, taking it happily. She shook Ben's hand, then pulled him closer, finishing with a friendly hug. "There. Now go back to that jerky girlfriend of yours."

Ben's eyes widened as if he'd been slapped.

"Just kidding!" Jessica recanted quickly, laughing to herself as Ben walked away down the sand.

*   *   *

"What do you think we ought to put here?" Stu asked Nina, pointing to the little box on the police report titled Description of Incident.

Nina glanced at the form impatiently, worried that all this paperwork was going to make her late for her shift at the beach. She raised her eyebrows in surprise, though, when she saw the tiny amount of space the form provided. "I don't know," she joked nervously. "Can you attach extra sheets?"

"This is a nightmare." Stu moaned. "Rachel is confusing enough without having to describe her in twenty words or less. Besides, I *never* did well on essay tests."

Nina watched from the chair next to Stu's as he bent back over the funky metal desk, his blond brows beetling with concentration. He began writing something, then stopped and chewed at the end of his pen.

"Hey, Nina!" a cheerful voice rang out suddenly from across the police station lobby. "Nina Harper, is that you?"

Nina turned around in her chair to see none other than Paul Jackson, her flame of the previous summer, striding toward her wearing an immaculate policeman's uniform. Paul had always been fussy about his clothes, and the rigidly starched, carefully pressed uniform with its highly polished shoes suited him to perfection. Nina took in the familiar face, the broad

212

shoulders, and felt her heart flutter excitedly.

"How are you?" he asked as their eyes connected.

"Good!" she replied, rising to her feet. "Wow, look at you. You're a police officer now."

"Yep. Graduated the academy with honors," Paul said proudly. "Not that I'm bragging or anything," he added with a wink and a flash of the killer smile that Nina remembered so well.

"That's great," she told him, feeling a little pang of remorse. Her biggest complaint about Paul the previous year had been his apparent lack of ambition. Had she ever been wrong about that! For a moment Nina felt sorry about what she'd left behind, but then she caught sight of Stu standing up on her left. *What am I thinking?* she asked herself as a rush of love welled up inside her. *Paul was nice, but Stu's incredible!*

"Uh, Paul, this is Stu Kirkwood," she stammered, introducing her old flame to her new. "Stu, Paul Jackson."

"Nice to meet you, Paul," Stu said affably, reaching out to shake Paul's hand. "Nina's told me all about you."

Paul's handsome face registered his surprise. "All good, I hope," he said, looking slightly uncomfortable.

"Of course!" Nina hurried to reassure him. "I think it's great that you decided to be a policeman."

"Yeah," Paul agreed, relaxing. "It *is* pretty

great. But hey, what are you guys doing here anyway? You didn't drop by just to see me."

Stu rolled his eyes. "You explain it," he said to Nina.

"You remember Rachel Max, right?" Nina asked Paul.

"Of course. Poor Rachel," Paul said sadly. "That woman's been through hell. Last summer, after she was arrested, no one came forward with the bail money, and she ended up having to stay in jail until her court date. By the time she finally went to trial, the fall semester had already started at the University of Chicago. Then she got probation, so she had to stay in California and couldn't go back to school." He shook his head. "Last summer really messed her up."

"Not just last summer," Nina said slowly, remembering the scene she'd witnessed the night before. "Anyway, Rachel was arrested last night."

"Not *again!*" Paul groaned. "What was it *this* time?"

"This time?" Nina echoed. The way Paul said it, he made it sound as if Rachel got arrested every day.

"She's been picked up a couple more times since last summer," Paul admitted reluctantly. "Shoplifting. She just can't seem to pull herself together. I've tried to help her, but she doesn't want anything to do with me now that I'm a policeman. She thinks I'm the enemy."

"Well, this was a little worse than shoplifting," Nina began. Then she told him the whole story.

"Wow," Paul exclaimed softly when Nina had finished. "It's even worse than I thought. She'll be going to County this time for sure."

"No," Nina corrected quickly. "We already talked to her social worker. Stu's going to pay to send Rachel to Collingswood Estate, to make sure she gets private counseling."

Paul's eyes went wide. "Collingswood!" he said with a low whistle and a sideways glance at Stu. "You must be rolling in it, man."

"I've got enough," Stu replied, clearly embarrassed. "I only want to help."

"Don't get me wrong! I think it's great," Paul hurried to clarify. "I can't imagine that Rachel won't get better at Collingswood. They've got the best of everything there."

"Yeah," said Stu. "That's what they tell me. Did you know they offer meditation too? I hope it works."

"Hey, Jackson!" An older officer had pushed the lobby door open just enough to stick his graying head inside. "Are we riding today or what?"

"Oops," Paul said quietly, wincing. "Be right there!" he yelled to the other officer. The older man nodded curtly and withdrew his head from the doorway.

"I've got to go," Paul told Nina hurriedly. "Patterson gets totally bent if I'm even a second

215

late. But hey, it was great to see you!"

"You too," Nina said, giving him a farewell hug.

Paul's strong arms wrapped around her in a way she remembered well. "It looks like you've got yourself a good man there," he whispered softly in her ear.

"Thanks," Nina said, smiling. "I know."

Paul broke off the embrace and with a rushed, apologetic grin hurried across the lobby to meet his partner.

"He seemed nice," Stu commented after Paul was gone.

"He *was* nice," Nina agreed. "But *you*," she added, turning to Stu with a smile. "You *are* nice."

"What's that supposed to mean?" Stu grinned. "That you're not finished with me yet?"

"I'm so far from finished with you that I'm not sure I've even started yet," Nina teased.

Stu made a face of mock terror. "I'm not sure if that's a promise or a threat."

"You'll have to wait and find out," Nina told him, trying to look mysterious. The effort was too much, though, and a moment later she broke down laughing. "I can't do this. One psycho per summer ought to be enough for any man."

Stu reached for her and pulled her into his arms. "It was *more* than enough for me," he said, sounding relieved to have the whole thing behind him. "What do you say we finish up this paperwork and get you off to the Main Tower?

216

Then tonight I think we ought to have a romantic dinner and make some plans for the rest of the summer."

"What kind of plans?" Nina asked, her heart suddenly pounding with anticipation.

"I don't really care," Stu said. "As long as they involve you and me and lots of time alone together."

Nina giggled. "You nut." She couldn't imagine anything she'd rather do than spend a lot of time alone with Stu. "I *do* have a new bikini you haven't seen yet," she added happily. "In case you want to factor that into your plans."

"Definitely," Stu agreed, his crystal blue eyes sparkling. "Wear it to dinner tonight."

Chapter
Fourteen

What time is it? Elizabeth wondered groggily, pushing herself away from Ryan on top of his still-made bed.

She'd fallen asleep in his arms the night before, after the two of them had cried themselves dry, but daylight was streaming through the half-closed blinds now, making her head hurt from the glare. The shouts of children playing in the sand outside drifted gradually into her consciousness. It must be late if people were already on the beach. *At least it's my day off,* she thought.

Moving quietly, Elizabeth rose and straightened out the twisted sweatsuit she still had on from the night before. Then she walked to the window, peering through the slats of the blinds at the scene outside. It was a beautiful day; the beach was already packed. Kids in bathing suits were everywhere, having the times of their lives.

Elizabeth sighed as she watched them play. Being that age seemed so simple to her now. How she wished she were back out in the sunlight instead of here in the dark with Ryan.

"Oooooh," Ryan groaned quietly from the bed. "My head!"

Elizabeth glanced in his direction, but he'd already pulled a pillow over his eyes and flipped onto his other side. *You're going to have to wake up sometime,* she told him silently. *And it'll still hurt just as much when you do.* With another sigh Elizabeth turned her attention back to the window. *Nina could probably use me this afternoon if I decided I wanted to work,* she thought, scanning the growing crowd. *It might be good to take my mind off of . . . hello!*

Elizabeth interrupted her own thoughts as a totally unexpected sight met her eyes. Jessica and Ben had just crossed into her line of vision, doing glass patrol together. Elizabeth watched with amusement as her sister pointed out item after item for Ben to pick up. Ben was not only doing all the picking up, but he was also holding the trash bag, Elizabeth noticed, smiling. It felt good to see Jessica and Ben on friendly terms again, and for a moment Elizabeth's spirits rose. *At least one good thing came out of last night.*

But the thought of the night before brought Elizabeth down with a bang. Patti was dead, and Ryan was in a lot of trouble. The police would probably be arresting him soon for his stunt with the rescue boat. In a way, that was the least of his problems. Ryan already had so many other things to answer for, so much weight on his shoulders. Elizabeth wondered if he was strong enough to face what he'd done—and what it had cost—and give up drinking too.

"My head feels like it's going to explode," Ryan complained suddenly, startling her out of her thoughts. He was awake now, sitting up on the rumpled bedspread.

"I'll get you some aspirin," Elizabeth offered. She turned toward the bathroom, but Ryan stopped her.

"No," he said, squeezing his head between his hands. "I want to feel this pain. I want to remember it for the rest of my life."

"You had quite a night last night," Elizabeth told him softly, returning to sit on the edge of the bed.

"I know." Ryan groaned. "*That's* what I'd like to forget." Rising unsteadily, he stumbled into the kitchenette and opened the utility cabinet, pulling out a half-full bottle of whiskey. "*There* you are," he whispered when he saw it.

"Ryan, no!" Elizabeth cried, rushing to his side. But Ryan simply twisted off the cap and poured the whiskey into the sink. Elizabeth stopped her steps abruptly, watching with relief as the amber liquid spiraled down the drain.

"This is the end of it," Ryan declared, throwing the empty bottle into the trash. "I have to do this. For Patti's sake." At the mention of Patti, Ryan's voice became choked, and Elizabeth knew how much he still hurt inside.

So this is what being scared sober is all about, she thought. But Ryan was still a long way from sober.

"This *isn't* the end of it," she told him, wishing it were. "It's a good beginning, but it's only a start."

"That's the kind of thing Patti used to say," Ryan said sadly. "I'm going to miss her so much."

"Me too," Elizabeth said softly, wrapping her arms around him.

He responded by pulling her toward him, hugging her fiercely. "I'm so sorry, Liz. I know I've caused you a lot of pain. Please believe that I never meant to hurt you. I . . . I tried to keep you away from me. From all of this."

"I know," she said. "I forgive you. But there's someone else you need to apologize to." She took his hand and led him to the window, pointing to where Jessica still patrolled the beach with Ben.

"Jessica." Ryan groaned. "Do you think she'll even speak to me?"

"There's only one way to find out," Elizabeth told him. "Come on. Let's go."

"Welcome to Café Winston!" Winston shouted, greeting Wendy and Pedro at the front

221

door of their beach house. He hustled them into the dining room almost before they'd had a chance to put down Pedro's suitcases. "Boy, I'm glad you guys came home this morning," he added, pointing toward the heaping dining table. "Even *I* couldn't eat that much food myself."

"I'm sure you'd give it your best shot, though," Wendy teased, glowing with happiness as Pedro pulled out a chair for her. She was wearing the slim pants she'd had on the night before, accompanied by one of Pedro's clean shirts.

"We'd have been crazy to eat at the hotel when Sweet Valley Shore's finest pancake chef is living right here in our house," Pedro said, smiling at Wendy. "Besides, you know what they say: There's no place like home." He took a seat next to his wife while Winston slid happily into a chair across the table.

"Wait till you see what I made this morning," Winston said proudly, taking the lids off the serving dishes. "Pancakes *and* waffles, bacon, sausage, strawberries with cream, and scrambled Egg-berts! Dig in, everyone."

"Dig in. Now *that's* romantic," Wendy commented dryly, a twinkle in her clear gray eyes. She whisked the dish full of strawberries away from Winston, placing it in front of Pedro instead.

"Oh, nice," Winston complained loudly. "Yesterday the berries were *all* for me. Today I don't get *any*."

Wendy blushed and kicked him under the table. *Watch yourself,* her gray eyes said.

"Aw, let Winston have the strawberries back," Pedro told her. "After all, he earned them last night."

"That's right, I did," Winston agreed, scooping a mountain of them onto his plate and covering them with whipped cream. "I'm thinking of going into the guru business, actually. It may be the only way I can get a job this summer. I'll call my venture Quacks-R-Us. What do you think?"

"I think I'm totally grateful for everything you did," Wendy replied, a mischievous gleam in her eyes. "And if I were you, I'd watch my back."

"Watch my back? What for?" Winston protested.

"No matter how noble the cause, you don't think I'm going to let you get away with tricking me like that, do you? I owe you one—that's all I'm saying."

"Me!" Winston exclaimed. "What about Pedro?"

Wendy laughed. "Like I really believe this was *Pedro's* idea. Sorry, Winnie, but this one has your name written all over it."

Winston grinned. Whatever Wendy had in store for him, he could take it. Besides, hadn't she just said she was totally grateful?

"Are you really looking for a job?" Pedro asked suddenly.

"Constantly." Winston groaned, his smile disappearing.

"I'll hire you if you want," Pedro offered. "I can always use another roadie."

"You mean go on tour with you?" Winston asked, his eyes becoming enormous.

"Sure. If you want to."

Did he *want* to? What kind of stupid question was that? Winston remembered the crazed crew of girls who had chased him and Pedro through the airport, and his heart beat wildly.

"Winston! Winston Egbert!" they shouted in his imagination.

"Sure, I can get you backstage," he told the cutest one. . . .

"If Winston's working for you, then who's going to stay with me?" Wendy complained, dumping cold water all over his fantasy.

But Pedro only smiled. "Actually I'd been meaning to talk to you about that. There's no way I'm leaving you behind this time. And you wouldn't want Winston to rattle around this big old house by himself for the rest of the summer, would you?"

"You want me to tour with you?" Wendy asked, looking uncertain. "Last time that didn't—"

"It's going to work this time," Pedro cut in, totally confident. "I had a long talk with my manager about it this morning. We'll have a private hotel suite in every city. You'll have a car and chauffeur to take you anywhere you want to go. And we'll spend time together every day. *Every* day, I promise."

"Oh, Pedro," Wendy said, happy tears welling up in her eyes. "That sounds like a dream come true."

"You mean I can do it?" Winston exploded excitedly. "Aw, *cool!*"

"You really think you're roadie material?" Wendy asked him, a slightly skeptical smile on her lips. "Those guys bust their butts, carrying all that heavy equipment around and everything."

"You just wait," Winston predicted confidently. "The Pedro Paloma show has never seen a roadie like Winston Egbert!"

"That's what I'm afraid of," Wendy told him, but Winston only beamed.

"Oops! There's another piece, Ben," Jessica said, pointing to something glinting in the sand. "Make sure you get it all."

Ben stooped to pick up the shard of glass Jessica had spotted, and Jessica smiled the moment his back was turned. "After this we should probably do a dog patrol," she told him, knowing who the one wielding the pooper-scooper would be.

"Great," Ben mumbled from his position on his hands and knees.

"Uh, Jessica, can I talk to you for a minute?"

Jessica whirled around, her stomach suddenly in knots when she saw Ryan, with Elizabeth standing beside him.

"What do you want to talk about?" Jessica asked, eyeing Ryan warily.

"You know. Last night." He glanced down at Ben. "Hey, Ben, would you mind giving us a couple of minutes alone?"

"With pleasure," Ben agreed, rising to his feet and handing Jessica the trash bag. "I've got to get back to my tower anyway. I'm sure *Miranda* will be happy to do dog duty with you," he said, a triumphant glint in his dark blue eyes.

So Ben wasn't completely beaten yet. Jessica smiled appreciatively as he turned and walked away down the beach. The rest of the summer lay before her.

But in the meantime there was Ryan. She turned to him with distaste. "I'm listening," she told him testily.

"Jessica, what I did to you was unforgivable," Ryan said without preamble, his voice intense. "All I can do is tell you I'm sorry."

"You and me both," Jessica replied sourly. She glanced covertly at her twin, wondering if Elizabeth would catch her double meaning— that she was sorry she'd had the fling with Ryan.

"Anyway, I hope that someday you'll be able to overlook all this. I'll do my best to make it up to you."

Jessica was unconvinced. "We'll see."

Ryan nodded, as if he understood her position. "I'm going to take a walk," he said, raising one hand to squeeze Elizabeth's shoulder briefly. "I've got a lot of things I need to work out."

"OK," Elizabeth agreed as Ryan strode away down the beach.

"*He* said a mouthful," Jessica observed as soon as Ryan was out of earshot. "Do you think he'll ever get his act back together?"

"I don't know," Elizabeth answered with a sigh. "I hope so. But hey, how are *you*, Jess?" she added in a happier tone. "Are you feeling all right today?"

Jessica shrugged. "I'm working on it. Thanks to you." Sudden tears filled her eyes as she remembered how close she'd come to dying the night before, alone in a dark, cold ocean. If it hadn't been for Elizabeth, she . . . she . . . she didn't even want to think about it. "Have I ever told you how lucky I am to have you for a sister?" Jessica asked, her voice breaking.

"Yeah," Elizabeth replied, laughing softly. "Only about once for every grain of sand on this beach."

Jessica flinched at her own predictability.

"Well, I really *mean* it this time," she covered. "Anyway, what about how lucky you are to have me? Did you ever stop to think what a boring place this world would be without me around to mess things up?"

Elizabeth shook her head. "You didn't mess anything up, Jess. I mean, not *this* time. We won't go into all the previous occasions right now."

"Very funny," Jessica retorted. But inside she was happy—deeply happy. She tossed her blond ponytail and let the smile on her mouth creep all the way up to her aquamarine eyes. Everything was better between her and Elizabeth and between her and Ben. Even Priya was acting human. Did it really matter in the grand scheme of things if her love life was in a tiny little slump?

Besides, that's so totally temporary, she told herself, confidence blossoming once again. *If I really put my mind to it, I bet I could find a new boyfriend by lunch.*

A lifeguard's whistle sounded suddenly to Jessica's right. Both girls whipped their heads around to see what was going on. Theo stood at the water's edge, cautioning some children who had gone out too far. The sun glinted off the oil on his dark skin, highlighting every muscle. Jessica watched as he waved the children in and then smiled at them when they reached the sand. He had perfect teeth, she realized suddenly, and his face had a chiseled, ruggedly handsome quality to it. He was a total hunk, actually. How come she'd never noticed before?

Well, she'd *noticed*, of course, but with everything that was happening in her life, she'd been too preoccupied to let it sink in. It was sinking in now, though. Sinking in in a big, big way.

"Theo sure is a great guy," Elizabeth observed. "He was a huge help last night."

"Yeah," Jessica agreed slowly. But she was really remembering how Miranda had made a special point of mentioning Theo's good looks and how little attention she'd paid. How could she have been so *blind*?

It was Ryan's fault, she told herself. *He and Ben had me totally distracted.* Thank goodness her head was all clear now! Jessica watched, mesmerized, as Theo walked along the shoreline, his eyes focused on the swimmers.

"You really ought to thank him for coming out last night and for driving you home and all," Elizabeth suggested. "I mean, if you feel up to it."

"Oh, I'm up to it," Jessica replied, a sly smile lighting her blue-green eyes. "I'm *completely* up to it, in fact."

"Jessica . . . ," Elizabeth began, catching on, but it was too late. Jessica was already trotting off across the sand, her sights fixed firmly on Theo. A little conversation, she'd laugh at his jokes, and the next thing she knew he'd be asking her out to dinner.

He's as good as mine, she thought, psyching herself up as she jogged. *What guy can resist the old Wakefield magic?* Jessica's smile grew broader by degrees.

"Watch out, Theo," she murmured, her feet skimming across the sand. "They say the third time's the charm!"

What other summer surprises lie in store for the Wakefield twins? Find out in Sweet Valley University #39, #40, and #41, arriving in stores June, July, and August 1998. In the meantime, don't miss Sweet Valley University #33: **OUT OF THE PICTURE.**

SIGN UP FOR THE
SWEET VALLEY HIGH®
FAN CLUB!

Hey, girls! Get all the gossip on Sweet
Valley High's® most popular teenagers
when you join our fantastic Fan Club!
As a member, you'll get all of this really
cool stuff:

- Membership Card with your own
  personal Fan Club ID number
- A Sweet Valley High® Secret
  Treasure Box
- Sweet Valley High® Stationery
- Official Fan Club Pencil (for secret
  note writing!)
- Three Bookmarks
- A "Members Only" Door Hanger
- Two Skeins of J. & P. Coats® Embroidery
  Floss with flower barrette instruction
  leaflet
- Two editions of *The Oracle* newsletter
- Plus exclusive Sweet Valley High®
  product offers, special savings,
  contests, and much more!

Be the first to find out what Jessica & Elizabeth Wakefield are up to by joining the
Sweet Valley High® Fan Club for the one-year membership fee of only $6.25 each
for U.S. residents, $8.25 for Canadian residents (U.S. currency). Includes shipping
& handling.

Send a check or money order (do not send cash) made payable to "Sweet Valley
High® Fan Club" along with this form to:

SWEET VALLEY HIGH® FAN CLUB, BOX 3919-B, SCHAUMBURG, IL 60168-3919

NAME_____
        (Please print clearly)

ADDRESS_____

CITY_____ STATE _____ ZIP_____
                                                        (Required)

AGE _____ BIRTHDAY_____ /_____ /_____

You'll always remember your first love.

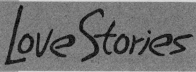

Looking for signs he's ready to fall in love?
Want the guy's point of view?
Then you should check out
the *Love Stories* series.
Romantic stories
that tell it like it is—
why he doesn't call,
how to ask him out,
when to say
good-bye.